AF430595

DARCY'S
ELUSIVE
BRIDE
A PRIDE & PREJUDICE VARIATION
GRACE SELLERS
ALLISON SMITH

THIS BOOK BELONGS TO:

Darcy pursues Elizabeth, who flees malicious rumors about a stormy night alone with Darcy, in order to protect Georgiana's betrothal. He gave her up once, he will not let another misunderstanding keep him from wedding the woman he has always loved.

Elizabeth, unaware of the depth of Darcy's regard, feels her only options are to wed a shopkeeper, or take a position as a companion. Heartbroken, she makes the practical choice.

But Darcy shows up for a ball at her employer's estate, having tracked her across the country, and she can no longer deny the truth of their feelings—or allow Lady Weatherstone to maneuver him into compromising her daughter, in order to force them to wed.

Darcy's Elusive Bride is a fast paced Pride & Prejudice sweet variation with a touch of angst, a midnight ball, a chase across London, and a warm Happily Ever After.

Darcy stared at the lovely golden-haired woman in front of him, her forehead creased in consternation.

"I am certain she will write to me once she is settled," Jane said, hands fluttering before they stilled, folding neatly onto her lap.

The fates were laughing at him. To hunt Elizabeth down, only to have missed her by a day.

But Jane Bennet would not meet his gaze.

"There cannot be so many agencies for impoverished ladies seeking employment," he said in a tight voice. "Surely you can recall which one." She claimed she did not know where Elizabeth was heading, citing a poor memory. He suspected that for her own reasons, she simply refused to tell him.

Her cheeks pinkened even further. "I know it must seem as if I am deliberately protecting my sister, but I assure you,

Mr Darcy, it is simply my poor memory. The children require so much attention—I find it difficult to recall details lately. It never occurred to me the need to memorise the name of her agency."

"Or of her employer."

"I am certain the name begins with an E. Lady Evelyn Whitestone or. . .perhaps Lady Anna Warston. The estate is a week's travel by carriage, and quite in the opposite direction of Longbourn, I do recall Lizzy was most pleased. . ." she trailed off.

"If you recall any details, you will inform me?" he asked.

She widened her eyes. Blue, innocent. . . false. "Of course! And as soon as she writes I will inform you."

He would not stand still waiting on this comedy of errors to come to a tragic conclusion. He would search London until he found that blasted agency. A week by carriage. . .she continued to slip through his fingers. But not forever, he vowed.

CONTENTS

There had been a time when a long walk in the morning mist would offer a resolution to any difficulty. That time had long since passed. She did not wish to marry a man she did not love because it was expedient.

What she wished mattered less than nothing.

Her home rose out of the mist, a ghost of the place it had once been. Elizabeth paused, steeling herself against a familiar stone in the pit of her middle. Former home, as she resided there on sufferance, companion to Longbourn's mistress.

Not for all the world would she have imagined two years ago that Charlotte would be the lady of Longbourn and Elizabeth, the second eldest daughter, would be a servant in her friend's household.

"Lizzy," Charlotte called from the breakfast room

as Elizabeth entered. "You were out in the rain again. Your hems will be caked in six inches of mud."

Elizabeth ignored the rebuke. The estate did not pay for her clothing, Elizabeth paid for it out of the small inheritance left her after the death of both her parents two years prior. So if her hems were caked in mud, the expense of replacing them was not Charlotte's concern.

"I will change and join you," Elizabeth said, voice neutral. Neutral was the best she could manage this morning, for a decision she did not desire to make loomed in front of her.

The sympathy in Charlotte's eyes only rubbed salt in the wound as Elizabeth entered the dining room a half hour later. "Do you wish to speak on it?"

Her friend meant well. After all, this was the exact same position Charlotte herself had been in when faced with the decision of whether to marry Collins.

"Discussing it makes it real," Elizabeth said, picking at a piece of bread on her plate.

Charlotte reached across the table and patted the top of her hand. "I know, and I am sorry for it. It is the lot of women to be forced to choose between two undesirable realities. But a choice must be made, Elizabeth, and not only for your future."

"I understand the situation." She kept the words polite, forcing herself to remain seated. Charlotte had said nothing wrong, and a display of temper would only brew tension in the household.

"Well, when you wish to confide in me, I am here." Charlotte pulled away when footsteps and the happy babble of a young child approached.

A maid appeared in the threshold with Annabelle, the firstborn child of Collins and his wife. At times Elizabeth felt a tiny twist of satisfaction that they did not yet have a son. Irony, that. But she should not feel so. She would not wish such an uncertainty on any woman, and after all, living here was not Charlotte's fault. She had simply made a wise decision, based on careful consideration of all available options. Though at the time Elizabeth had scorned her reasoning, pride always crumpled before a fall.

Elizabeth now understood full well the uncertainty of being a woman past the first blush of youth, living on the precarious charity of relatives and facing the long, bleak years of a cloudy existence.

She could not stay in such spirits for long, though. Little Annabelle babbled, reaching out chubby arms to Elizabeth, who took her with a delighted smile. Charlotte looked on serenely, a smile on her lips. Truly, wife and motherhood suited her well.

"There are benefits to marriage," Charlotte said softly, "even if at first you do not feel great affection for your husband."

Looking at the child in her lap, Elizabeth could not

disagree. No matter how distasteful the thought of the act to produce a child with a man she did not love, the results were undeniable.

"Yes, you are the most beautiful, cheerful little girl on the earth," Elizabeth said with a smile that softened her expression, cradling the squirming toddler close to her chest. "And well worth the. . .inconvenience."

She glanced at Charlotte, who met her eyes, a pained expression on her face. Elizabeth grinned, and they both laughed.

The clouds dissipated by afternoon. To escape the house, Charlotte and Elizabeth left Annabelle in the care of her nurse and walked into town on the pretext of examining cloth for some new gowns for the child who grew out of one as fast as another could be sewn.

They linked arms at the elbow, much like they had as younger women. "What else can you do if you do not accept Mr Langston, Lizzy? I know he is not ideal, but he has a steady income."

"He is a shopkeeper. It would be marrying down."

"Perhaps." They had had this discussion many times. "But he is not a *poor* shopkeeper, and with your guidance you may help him do what my father did, who is now a Sir."

Elizabeth sighed. "It's not my life's purpose to be

any man's ambition. I want a life and pursuits of my own."

"You still think like a girl, Lizzy." Charlotte pressed her arm, taking the sting out of the words. "Jane is courting a—"

"A solicitor. Not a shopkeeper."

"A solicitor is still not a gentleman. Lydia has wed an officer. Mary is happy as a companion to your aunt's children. It is only you and Kitty left to be settled."

"Are you so eager to see me go?"

"Of course not. But I worry. Come, we'll say no more of it. There is nothing I can say that you have not already thought of. I know in time you will make the sensible decision."

Sensible. In other words, accept the proposal of a man she did not love, just a decade shy of an age old enough to be her father. Sensible, because he would provide a home, food, clothing, respectability. Perhaps contentment, if not happiness, once she had children.

She did not want sensible, however. She wanted love. She wanted. . .Elizabeth sighed. What she wanted did not matter. If she were intelligent, she would focus solely on what was within her grasp and forgo the silly daydreams of youth.

"How can a woman maintain her integrity," she murmured, "if she weds a man she cannot love in exchange for security?"

Elizabeth sat alone in the sitting room, pulling a needle too quickly through her embroidery fabric, stopping short when she felt a sharp pinprick in her finger.

Blast.

She'd inadvertently—stupidly—stuck the end of a finger with the needle. A red rivulet of blood swelled from it, and she muttered words to herself she should not be using. But she was all alone. If one was going to curse, drawing blood seemed a proper opportunity to do so.

She stuck her finger in her mouth to clean the blood away. Putting one's bleeding appendage in one's mouth was bad form, but Elizabeth found it difficult to care about what was unladylike at this juncture in her life. An old memory rose in her mind: the tiny bloody fingerprints that stained her and Jane's first kits as they learned to embroider many years ago. She and Jane had giggled whenever Mama left the room as they pointed their small, blood pricked fingers toward each other and squealed. The memory was pleasant. How she missed Jane's steady presence now.

Her finger now clean, she took up the needle and pulled it through before she stopped again.

She still had one unmarried, unfettered sister: Kitty.

She would take Kitty and travel. . .where? Where was close enough to go but still far enough away to feel different?

Lambton, where Aunt Gardiner was from.

She needed to go away, and a trip to Lambton would allow her to take herself and Kitty out of Charlotte's—and Collin's—way for a few days. She had a friend in Lambton, Mrs Fischer. She and Kitty could stay with her. She stabbed through the fabric a third time, pulling the yarn tightly, not puncturing herself this time.

Yes, Lambton would do well. It would provide her time to think things through. To consider Mr Langston and her own life. Elizabeth set the embroidery next to her on the loveseat. She was never overly fond of embroidery, anyway.

She would tell Charlotte presently.

His sister sat in front of him, hands folded demurely in her lap. Darcy wondered if she positioned herself in front of the tall window on purpose, all the better for the sunlight to highlight her angelic golden beauty.

"Georgiana, it was not my intent to issue an ultimatum, but it seems as if you do not understand the consequences of your actions."

She looked up, eyes a stormy grey, belying the

serene pose she presented. "I understand conse-quences. I also understand free agency."

"You read too many books." A sentence he had never thought to hear come out of his mouth, considering the import he placed on reading for the improvement of a person's mind, whether male or female. "Lord Randolph encourages you."

Which worried Darcy. One had hoped a husband would be a calming influence on his sister, but she had fallen in love with the one peer in England who was bored by biddable, quiet ladies.

Georgiana rose. "You mean to say that my education has exposed me to ideas considered radical for a woman of my station in life. My fiancée enjoys a good debate. He says it keeps his mind sharp."

He sighed. "Lord Randolph does you a disservice. There is yet the possibility his father will not approve of the match. Until the duke gives his blessing—"

"Yes, yes, I understand. There must be no whiff of scandal. John has already explained how his father is." A small, mocking smile played on her lips. "Very well, brother. I shall strive to maintain the dignity of Pemberley in a more traditional manner. I will be on my best behaviour when he and his parents arrive."

"No more luncheons with journalists, no more protests, no more attendance of salons hosted by women of. . .independent means."

Her brow arched, an impish glint in her eyes. "Independent means. How diplomatic."

His teeth ground. "Nevertheless."

Georgiana held up a hand. "I *understand,* Fitzwilliam. You needn't threaten me again."

"For at least another three months," he muttered under his breath as she glided out of the sitting room. That was about how long the effects of his lectures usually lasted before he was pulling her out of another wild scrape. One day she would go too far and he would be unable to salvage her reputation. Despite the understanding between her and Lord Randolph, until he had his father's blessing, no official announcement could be made.

The duke should be pleased for Georgiana to wed his son, considering the size of her dowry and the rumours that the duke's estate was impoverished. But he was a notorious, haughty elitist who cut anyone with even the slightest hint of scandal to their name. Duke Randall was known to want a girl of blemishless reputation for his heir.

Darcy grimaced. Georgiana's past was hardly blemishless. If only she would stop running off her companions, though the last one had been so painfully insipid Darcy could not blame her. No, she needed an older woman with wit and a pleasant demeanour who was nonetheless close enough in age Georgiana did not feel as if she was being chaperoned by a maiden aunt.

The solution had been obvious the entire time, of course, Darcy had simply been reluctant. It was not that Georgiana needed a companion. No, *he* needed a *wife.*

A woman of beauty and breeding to match his sister's energy, who could set a suitable example of stylish yet dignified conduct. Yet he pined over a woman he could not have.

Kitty lagged behind Elizabeth as they walked the distance from Lambton to the outskirts of the lands surrounding Pemberley, complaining nearly every step.

"It's going to rain," Kitty said dramatically, glancing up at the sky through the trees.

Elizabeth ignored her sister's protestations and strode toward a patch of flowers that bloomed where the trees thinned. Since coming to Lambton, her feet had itched to walk the beautiful landscape—and not only because walking these lands made her feel closer to him.

"Keep up," Elizabeth called back. "We're nearly there. I'll pick you a lovely bouquet of wildflowers."

"You know they make me sneeze." She sniffled loudly to prove it.

"You may have the first bath when we return." Elizabeth slipped between tall, ancient trees that twisted skyward. Was there anything as magnificent as an English forest? "It's marvelous, isn't it?"

Kitty sneezed. "I dearly wish you would discard this habit of taking long walks when you need to think. Thinking is rarely beneficial to a woman. Just marry Mr Langston and be done with it. Will you finally accept his proposal when we return home?"

Elizabeth still hadn't decided. Whether she would wed Mr Langston, or even if she would return to Longbourn. She swallowed, ignoring the hitch in her throat.

She would not weep.

She'd promised herself that. No matter what.

They'd all been through too much.

There were far worse things in life than marrying a decent, secure man. And, of course, thinking of Mr Langston could not help but dredge up memories of another man, a gentleman whom she might have married if only she had been wiser, less proud.

She banished those thoughts. She had sworn she would never regret what had passed, but look to the future. Elizabeth plucked a flower, its stem popping with a satisfying snap.

"Look, Kitty, there are daisies here." A moment later, Kitty cried out. Elizabeth whirled, dashing the few paces to her sister.

"Oh, bother," Kitty said, biting her lip. "Help me up, Lizzy. I tripped over a stupid root."

Elizabeth held out her hands to grasp Kitty's, her brow furrowing. "Your face is pale. Did you turn your ankle?"

Kitty took Elizabeth's hands, attempting to rise. Her lips thinned as she gingerly placed weight on the injured ankle.

Elizabeth sighed. "I see. Well, there's no help for it. We're too far from town for you to wait here alone while I seek help. Loop your arm around my neck and hobble."

"It will take us all day to return," Kitty complained.

"They may send someone for us." But Elizabeth did not hold out hope, not when her penchant for long, meandering walks was well known. No one would be alarmed if they were a few hours late.

Elizabeth set her jaw, knowing there was no choice but to continue moving forward. She kept a close eye on the forest path, not wanting a repeat of the stumble, and they made very slow progress. Poor Kitty was biting her lip in pain, her ankle likely swelling in the boot. Elizabeth prayed they did not have to cut the boot off. The cost of a new pair if the leather could not be repaired. . .

Horse hooves behind them warned Elizabeth of an oncoming traveller.

"Thank goodness!" Kitty exclaimed. "Hopefully it is a handsome gentleman."

Elizabeth hoped their luck ran to a gentleman at all, handsome or no. They limped to the side of the path and waited as the hooves approached. This was Pemberley land, or at least the outskirts of it, so it could not be anyone dangerous. Her heartbeat skipped, as a stray thought whispered that as they were on Pemberley lands, there was always a chance she might see *him* again.

As she struggled not to *feel*, a man approached on a chestnut stallion, his dark riding clothes both elegant and severe, the sombre attire of a gentleman who disdained fashion in favour of dignity. Dark hair, a trifle longer than current fashion dictated, brushed the edge of his crisp cravat. His seat on the horse demonstrated ease and mastery, his back straight with youthful strength.

Elizabeth inhaled sharply. She knew this man. She would know him anywhere. And she had mere moments to mask her surge of longing and compose herself to some form of pleasant indifference.

He seemed to notice the women and spurred his horse forward, pulling up and looking down with piercing blue eyes. Elizabeth looked down at the ground as if to hide from him.

"May I be of assistance?" he asked, voice deep and even. Reserved, as she remembered, though not quite displeased. This was not a dance, as it was the last time she had seen him, after all. He was at home here, in these forests. Then he frowned. "Elizabeth Bennet?"

Darcy. It was as if her struggles not to think of him called him out of the forest. "My sister stumbled and turned her ankle, sir," she said softly, embarrassed by how his presence sped her heart. Thank heavens he had no idea.

Stay calm.

The polite neutrality of his expression shifted into incredulousness. "Whatever are you doing. . .here?"

Elizabeth did not take offense at his open astonishment. The Bennet girls were the last people he would have expected to see on his travels today. He stared at her, the directness of his gaze unabashed.

She felt warmth in her cheeks. "We are visiting a friend in Lambton."

Darcy dismounted, approaching slowly. He stopped, closer than polite social distance dictated, and looked down at her. "Pemberley is not far from here. You should have come to me."

He could not mean 'me' in a personal sense, despite the undercurrent in his tone. The subtle weight of shared tempestuous history.

. . .I love you, albeit against my will, and have reconciled I will take no other woman to wife.

They had not parted on the best of terms two years ago. Not the best of terms at all.

I will spare you the agony of inflicting such shameful relations on you, sir. I could never wed a man who loved me against the dictates of his intellect.

"We're unfamiliar with these woods," she said. "I did not realise your home was so near. And I did not want to leave my sister alone while I sought help."

He nodded. "I understand. Forgive me, is Miss Elizabeth still the correct address?"

How could she have forgotten the clear, captivating blue of his eyes? But she had not forgotten. She had shoved the memory as far down as possible, underneath layers of regret she refused to acknowledge.

"It is Miss Elizabeth," she said. "I am. . .my situation has not changed."

With sudden clarity she knew that she never would, for having refused this man, how could she accept someone lesser? It would not be fair to Mr Langston to marry him and spend the rest of her days withholding the true depths of her regard and affection because in her eyes he fell so far short.

"I see," he said, then looked at Kitty. "Miss. . .do I have permission to lift you onto the horse?"

Kitty was staring at him with wide eyes. At least her sister's mouth was not wide open.

"Oh, of course, sir," she said, voice breathless. She smiled, her sweetest and most innocently flirtatious expression. "I am Kitty, though I do not expect you to have recalled. I was sooo much younger then."

Elizabeth cringed, then cleared her throat. "I appreciate your assistance, Mr Darcy. I will follow behind. Do not trouble to slow your pace on my account."

"Do not be ridiculous. After Miss Kitty is on the horse, then you may mount behind her. I will walk at his side and ensure you make it safely to town. That is where you are staying?"

"Yes, indeed, but I would not dream of—"

Darcy sighed. "You have not changed," he cut her off. "As quick to debate as ever. One might have hoped you would mellow with age."

Her mouth snapped shut. Then, surprising them both, Elizabeth laughed. The shameless impertinence of the man. "No, but you could not have hoped for so much, Mr Darcy."

If her laugh had surprised him, his sudden, warm smile was as unexpected in its measure. "No, I could not have, could I? But then I did not dare hope to see you again at all, Miss Elizabeth."

***

Unfortunately, it was not a long walk, though he imagined it would have been for two women, one of them injured. Still, he walked slower than usual. Darcy needed to think.

Miss Elizabeth Bennet.

For over two years it had taken conscious work not to think about her when he rose in the morning, when he settled into bed at night. Not to allow the anger and craving twist into bitterness.

His first love and his first heartache twined into one.

If it had not been for the determined cheerfulness of his sister's company, he might have allowed cynicism to make of him a man he did not desire to be.

He led his horse on and tried not to allow his conflicting feelings to show.

"How have you been?" he asked her, glancing up at the women on the horse.

Elizabeth's seat was lovely. She rode with a straight back and serene expression that he recalled, looking straight ahead. The younger one, whom he remembered as being as incorrigible as her other sister of similar age, sat with a pinched expression. She was in pain, which could account for her lack of incessant chatter. Or perhaps time had matured her? Doubtful.

After a moment Elizabeth glanced down, dark eyes not as inscrutable as she might have wished. In the tilt of her head, the set of her shoulders, was the same studied neutrality he attempted now to project.

So, she was not unaffected.

"I am well."

Her low, reserved tones wove through him. After a time he had stopped straining to remember the timbre of her voice. Stopped telling himself that he could end the obsession by traveling to see her one last time. Perhaps she regretted her decision as much as he regretted his pride. Pride that had been the last lingering, crumbling remnant of youth. But he was past all that now. What a fool he had been then.

Only a complete ass would have approached the woman he claimed to love so cavalierly, too convinced of his own importance. The last years had taught him, and retaught him, much about manhood.

"And yourself?" she asked. "I trust your sister has been in good health?"

"Excellent health and spirits," he replied, internally grimacing at the banality of their conversation. They danced around each other, and he despised such games. "Your family?"

Darcy tensed, knowing he had erred when her expression darkened and she looked away.

"My father passed, and my mother," she said after a moment.

If he were a little less in control of himself, he would have missed a step. "I am grieved for your loss." His mind whirled. Her father dead? Then that self-important cousin of hers must have inherited the estate. She said she had not wed. "You are still at Longbourn?"

Elizabeth smiled humourlessly.

"Oh, there is nowhere else to go," Miss Kitty said,

jolting Darcy out of the illusion that he and Elizabeth were alone. He had forgotten about Kitty's presence.

"Kitty," Elizabeth said.

"Well, it is no use—"

"Kitty," she said more sharply.

Darcy sympathised and also saw with some amusement that the younger sister was little better behaved than before. Well, perhaps a bit better—she had not been chattering the entire time they walked. One thing he understood was how time changed people.

"Kitty and I are still at Longbourn. Jane is with our aunt and Lydia has wed. Mary—" she stopped abruptly.

He suppressed a rising brow. Was the other sister dead? He waited. She would tell him or not.

"Mary has found a satisfactory situation."

Ah. The fate of poor gentlewomen who did not wed. How was it Elizabeth had escaped such a life? Could she be betrothed? He changed the subject, attempting to show he cared about her life—which he did, cared more than he wished to admit to himself.

"And your friend? Forgive me, I forget her name."

"Oh, that's Charlotte," Kitty said. "You will never guess! I should make you guess, it would be amusing, but I will not. Charlotte is married to cousin Collins. Can you imagine?"

Darcy glanced between the sisters. "I. . .see. A

respectable match." For Mrs Collins. A practical woman, and elegantly behaved, he recalled.

"Indeed," Elizabeth said, voice drier than summer brush. "We were delighted to welcome her into the family."

During his brief stay at Netherfield he had come to appreciate Elizabeth's particular form of self-deprecating, if slightly impertinent, wit. She was not a traditional beauty, but as time passed her large, darkly lashed eyes and glossy hair drew him. She had a natural elegance in her bearing, different from Caroline's more studied grace. Yes, he had found himself fascinated, reluctantly attracted. She had been, however, the second daughter of a poor gentleman. If Darcy had been inclined to overlook her lack of fortune, he had not quite been able to overlook her sometimes crass family. He'd been such a self-important fool, who'd foolishly bungled what should have been the day that led to him claiming happiness for the rest of his life. But no, he'd shut up like a clam instead. For many reasons.

The difficulty of managing one exuberant, barely restrained sister already rested with the weight of a noose around his neck. He could only imagine how Georgiana might have been influenced by the younger Bennet girls, whose complete lack of decorum in public drew many an askance eye and whispered opinion.

No, no matter how pleasing he found Miss Elizabeth's company, at the time he had thought he could not afford for her sisters to exacerbate Georgiana's willfulness. He'd wanted Elizabeth, but had insisted she disentangle herself from her family. Now that Georgiana had met Lord Randolph, it seemed his caution was correct.

Foolish, arrogant.

But George had torn into him when after months he had finally revealed the story. She was the only person to whom he could confide, and she had been heartily tired of his ill mood.

"You said what?" She stared at him, aghast. "How could you expect her to agree to such a thing? Abandon her family?"

"Not abandon——" he began stiffly.

"Do not play word games with me, William. Argh! You are so vexing! The first woman you have ever proposed to— finally some hope of seeing you wed and you muck it up. You could never even love a woman who would agree to shun her family, so why would you have asked it?"

He glanced up at Elizabeth, his sister's words ringing in his mind. Her gaze flickered down towards him and her lips curled in a polite smile before she resumed watching the path back toward Lambton.

In too brief a time they reached the townhome, directed by Elizabeth's low murmur of instructions. A woman came out, a hand on her chest.

"Mr Darcy! And Elizabeth, whatever…"

He helped Elizabeth dismount, her soft hand in his for far too brief a moment. She nodded her thanks and turned to the woman.

"Kitty has injured her ankle. Mr Darcy happened upon us on our walk and so kindly offered to escort us home."

Darcy assisted Kitty down from the horse. She smiled at him, despite her pale face, and he was uncertain whether the brush of her lithe body against his was an accident. He released her, taking a careful step back.

An older man, the woman's husband perhaps, emerged and immediately came to assist Kitty.

"Thank you so much, Mr Darcy," Kitty said in a husky voice, lowering her eyes coyly. "It was sooo gallant of you. I shall never forget."

He bowed, expression carefully distant. "No thanks are needed, Miss Kitty. I would do the same for any gentlewoman in distress."

Her laughter was a tinkle, grating on his nerves because he was certain she meant for it to be light and feminine. "Oh, but not every woman is gentle, is she?"

"Kitty, let us get you inside and not take up any more of Mr Darcy's time," Elizabeth said, voice crisp.

She turned to him with a small curtsy, back perfectly erect. "Please accept my thanks as well." Her expression lightened, a familiar flash of humour in her eyes. "I would say I hope to return the favour, but I do not think I could lift you onto a horse should you turn your ankle."

"I might be tempted to do so, and lay awaiting rescue in the forest, if only to enjoy the sight of you trying, Miss Elizabeth," was his grave response.

He executed a bow to match her own, seeing her slight smile out of the corner of his eye as he turned. Then she was away, speaking in refined tones that managed to fall just short of commanding, while maintaining a woman's feminine softness.

As he mounted his horse, he turned to catch another brief look at her, but the group had already entered the house.

Fate had thrown Elizabeth Bennet into his path once again. It was up to him to determine what to make of the opportunity.

CHAPTER THREE

"It was sooo romantic," Kitty gushed. "Mr Darcy is a prince of a man. He carried me in his arms."

He had done no such thing. "Kitty, cease this nonsense," Elizabeth said, irritated. She turned to Mrs Fischer. "I will stay with my sister to ensure she is comfortable. There is no need for you to tend her."

"Nonsense, you are here to visit, not to spend your time ensconced in a sick room."

"I am injured, not sick," Kitty said. "And I do not intend to be in this bed for very long. The prospect utterly bores me."

Elizabeth was of the mind that confinement to a bedroom would do her sister a world of good. Though time had mellowed Kitty's exuberant nature some, she still was not as guarded as Elizabeth would like, especially considering their situation in life. Lydia was safely wed, but Elizabeth lived in dread of the day Kitty lost patience with decorum and common sense and made a fool of herself, ruining her chances for any kind of match.

If she ruined herself, not even a shopkeeper would offer for her.

She pushed the inevitable thoughts of Mr Langston aside. The purpose of this trip was to help her gain clarity on her path forward in life, but the longer she was away from Longbourn, the less she desired to even consider the match. It was liberating to be away from the Collinses and the burden she felt whenever Charlotte's eyes were on her. She yearned, desperately, for another option. Her thoughts spun a tangled skein the rest of the evening.

Kitty fell asleep, having grudgingly resigned herself to the enforced pampering. Elizabeth put away the playing cards, then settled onto the window seat, much like she might have in her own bedroom at home.

A soft knock on the door drew her attention. Mrs Fischer poked her head in, then entered.

"I have a note for you, dear," she said. "A boy from Pemberley brought it by."

Elizabeth's window faced away from the front of the house, so she would not have seen a messenger approach. She rose, eyes fixed on the envelope in Mrs

Fischer's hands. What could it be? No one besides Darcy would know to write to her.

She hesitated a moment before taking it, then told herself to stop being foolish.

"Thank you," she said.

"I'll have a hot toddy sent up." Curiosity lit Mrs Fischer's eyes, but she left the room, allowing Elizabeth her privacy.

Elizabeth opened the note, skimming the contents. It was indeed Mr Darcy. He inquired after Kitty, expressed his desire to see her mended, and offered a physician in the morning—apologising for the delay as the man was currently called away on another matter. The tone struck by the note was one of neighbourly but carefully brisk distance.

But he signed it, *Yours, Fitzwilliam Darcy.*

She folded the note and set it aside. The ending salutation meant nothing, and only a silly woman would read some lingering trace of affection where there was none. A silly woman or a desperate one. If she had accepted Darcy's proposal, how different would her life have been? She could have wed him and over time brought him around to the tolerance, if not affection, of her family. She should have been like Charlotte—wise, patient.

Elizabeth could now admit that she had been as foolish in her own way as Lydia had ever been.

By the next day Elizabeth was more than ready to

leave the house. She banished Mr Darcy from her mind, after all it was unlikely she would see him again and entertaining any pangs of what might have been would only torment her. No matter how stimulating their past conversations, no matter how she thought she had seen him look at her with the glint of banked fire in his eyes those short years ago—that time was gone.

The fantasy of a rich, handsome, intelligent man her age to come and rescue Elizabeth from a life of drudgery was the stuff of fairy tales, and only children or wealthy noblemen's daughters entertained them with any seriousness.

Elizabeth walked into town, determined to raise her spirits by a visit to the baker to choose a treat. Though it would not do to habitually soothe herself with sweets, every once in a while would do no harm. She was in no danger of becoming a plump shopkeeper's wife yet.

As she was about to reach for the handle of the white washed entrance, it flew open. Elizabeth snatched her hand away and took a hasty half hop back to avoid being bowled over by whomever had so exuberantly thrown open the door.

A young woman stepped out, gold curls in wisps around her face, cheeks flushed a becoming shade of pink as if she had just enjoyed a good laugh—or a good row.

It was the second time this week Elizabeth had run into a Darcy. "Miss Darcy!"

She curtsied, stepping further out of the girl's way. It was difficult not to think of her as a girl, for all she must be a young woman now, after two years. But if Georgiana had not changed since they had first met at Pemberley—and Elizabeth thought it unlikely—then she would be just as much a devil-may-care as any of Elizabeth's own sisters.

Blue eyes widened. "Why, I know your face. Wait. . .do not tell me." Her brow furrowed. "Oh, I am horrible with names, but I never forget a face."

Elizabeth smiled. There was something charming about Georgiana's unabashed admission to having completely forgotten her name. "Shall I give you a hint?"

"Miss Elizabeth!" she squealed. "I would know that smile and voice anywhere! You always sounded like a mischievous governess. I could not quite decide which, so I decided upon both."

"I am certain I have been called worse."

Georgiana ignored her dry tone, linking arms at the elbow, much like Charlotte or Jane would have done. She felt a pang, missing them both, but more than anything missing Jane.

"Come, tell me whatever are you doing in Lambton? My dreadful brother has not allowed me back to Meryton—something about officers and temptation, though I am sure I do not know what he meant at all. I longed to see you, of course. And your sister, the one with beauty to rival my own."

Unabashed and lacking false modesty. Yet the combination did not turn Elizabeth away. How could it, when underneath was a wry, self-deprecating humour much like her brother?

"I am visiting friends in town. We will be here a few more days, my sister Kitty and I."

Miss Darcy pressed a hand against her pursed lips. "Kitty? Kitty. . .ah, yes. The one who so loves to dance. The other was quite enamoured of a handsome man in a red coat, if I recall."

"Your recollection is flawless. Lydia is now wed to such a red coat."

"Marvelous. Oh, but you and your sister must come to dinner this week. My brother has me on a veritable house arrest. I am not allowed to linger in town, and he has threatened to set a gorgon on me as a guard if I do not comply. I am *so* bored for stimulating company."

"Well, I would be happy to be of service and do my part to ease your boredom."

Even as she said it her mind batted at her. What was she doing, accepting such an invitation? She would have to see Darcy, speak to Darcy. . .pretend to be unaffected by Darcy. That he did not hate her or at least merely disdain her was a miracle. And yet she had seen and heard neither of those two emotions in his voice, nor the shadows in his eyes. She had not seen or heard much, for his thoughts were sealed up as ever behind an impenetrable brick wall.

Miss Darcy spoke again, in a lowered voice. "I do have an ulterior motive for the invitation. A special gentleman will be coming to dine as well, with his parents, and an announcement might be made if they approve of me."

"How could any gentleman's parents not approve of you?" Elizabeth cried in a hushed tone, conscious of the listening ears of people they passed.

Georgiana gave her a tremulous smile. "There are reasons. They are conscious of their rank and dignity, and I am not as politely behaved as they might wish for their son and heir."

"Nonsense. Any family would be fortunate to welcome a daughter with such talent, grace, and beauty." Elizabeth was not attempting to ingratiate herself. She felt genuine indignation on Miss Darcy's behalf, sensing in the younger woman a core of uncertainty that could only come of having been told she was not good enough. But who would do so?

Miss Darcy's cheeks bloomed with pink. "If only Lord Randolph's parents were certain to share your good opinion."

"I am sure they shall once they meet you." Elizabeth reached for her hand and squeezed, thrilled for Georgiana even as her own ever present wistfulness rose in her throat. "So, another woman present to help ease one's nerves?"

"You understand."

"I do." She worried briefly about the gowns she had packed, then dismissed the thought. She would be going to lend Miss Darcy her emotional support—the state of her dress was irrelevant.

Georgiana's hands clasped together. If she had heard the irony in Elizabeth's tone, she ignored it. "Perfect. I will send a carriage for you. We will have a fabulous time."

CHAPTER FOUR

"You did what?" Darcy turned and stared at his sister.

Her look was impatient. "Invited the Bennet sisters to dinner."

Upon hearing Georgiana say the name Bennet, Caroline Bingley's head nearly swiveled off her neck.

"Good God," Caroline said. "How will they dress? The last I heard, they were living in penury. That cannot be conducive to a wardrobe fit for society."

Darcy frowned. He had not heard such, but Caroline lived at Netherfield, though sometimes he wondered if she had moved into Pemberley and no one had informed him. Georgiana seemed to enjoy her company in an odd kind of way, so he said nothing. "What do you mean?"

She snapped the book she was not reading closed,

a certain sign she was about to settle into a long diatribe of gossip. He had a feeling he would regret giving into her entreaty to invite her to Pemberley to visit with Georgiana.

"Their father and horrid mother died some years ago, and the sisters were all forced to find arrangements elsewhere since the heir moved into the home with his new wife. I believe Miss Elizabeth is yet unwed, but I cannot imagine she will suffer that state for long. There was talk of a shopkeeper." Amused malice flashed in her eyes. "I hear he is tolerably well off. In her circumstances, a woman cannot afford the luxury of choice. Especially when one has no other suitors."

The news struck him in a way he would examine later, in privacy. Elizabeth, living in penury on the charity of relations and perhaps forced into an unwanted engagement with a man who was beneath her? He could not imagine a more undignified fate for a woman with her intelligence and beauty.

For a moment he resented her. She could have been *his* wife. Was this fate what she had chosen over burying her pride and accepting how unfit her family was for the upper echelons of society? He had intended to take her away, provide her the accoutrements fit for a woman with her natural grace. The shopkeeper obviously knew he had a diamond hidden in a lump of coal.

"That is unfortunate," he said. "Georgiana, of course you must invite the sisters to dinner. I am certain you will enjoy their company."

As would he. He covered his introspection by pretending to read the paper in front of him.

Georgiana gave him a sidelong glance. "I seem to recall you also enjoyed the company of Miss Elizabeth. Or rather enjoyed engaging her in verbal battle."

"I did no such thing." Caroline did not know of the failed proposal, but of course his sister would tease him unmercifully. "Why *did* you invite them?"

"I like Miss Elizabeth. She is very witty, and always laughing at everyone, though you would not know it because she is so clever. It *would* be a shame were she to wed a shopkeeper. Surely she must have at least one other prospect."

Darcy ignored his sister. She was needling him on purpose, he knew it.

Caroline made an inelegant sound. "Really. A poor, plain woman who laughs at everyone else around her? I do not see the appeal, and I never shall. The other sister was tolerable, but Miss Elizabeth I found disagreeable."

Georgiana frowned briefly at Caroline. "I suppose this means you have not had her over to Netherfield in the last years. I wonder you found her disagreeable. Could it be because you were unable to bait her the way you do those you think beneath you? She is much too strong minded for your usual games."

Caroline inhaled sharply, prepared to retort.

Darcy hastily interjected. "That is enough, Georgiana. Do not be uncivil." Though secretly, he agreed.

His sister sniffed, smoothing her expression and giving him her sweetest smile. "I, uncivil? Never. Though is tea too much to ask?"

"I will make a point," Caroline replied in a voice laden with sarcasm, "when I return to Netherfield, to invite Miss Elizabeth over for tea if that will please you."

"It will. It will, indeed. For if *I* was able to avail myself of Miss Elizabeth's presence anytime I chose, I would do so. And know of at least one other person who shares my opinion."

Darcy stared hard at his sister. She strayed perilously close to disclosing a truth he preferred to keep to himself. Did Georgiana really like Elizabeth that much? And should he not take advantage of her amiable feelings and encourage the two women to spend time together? While Elizabeth's opinions were as strong as Georgiana's, they were also tempered with maturity and kindness.

Thoughtfully, he began to plot how he might persuade Elizabeth to spend more time with his sister while in Lambton, ignoring the mocking voice in the back of his mind informing him he was simply attempting to see more of Elizabeth himself. She was just the sort of companion Georgiana needed—someone to exert a calming, graceful influence over Georgiana. Perhaps Elizabeth's presence at dinner would assure Lord Randolph's father as to Georgiana's character for choosing so sensible and well-mannered a friend.

In the back of his mind was the thought that Elizabeth should have been far more than a suitable friend. She should have been his wife, the one to help wisely guide Georgiana these last two years and counter some of his sister's fierier impulses. With cold clarity, Darcy acknowledged that he could *still* have Elizabeth to wife. If her situation was as desperate as Caroline intimated, then Elizabeth would be a fool to turn him down, and he knew she was no fool. Two years ago she had not thought herself in any desperate straits, and perhaps hoped she might receive other offers—before disaster struck with the deaths of her parents.

Did he really want her to marry him because she had no choice?

But if he could have the woman he wanted, did he care? In time, she would grow to love him and value their life together. He was certain of it. He had never wanted to be wed for his fortune, however.

Such thoughts had to be set aside with the arrival of Lord Randolph. Darcy focused on the latest guest, and the reason for this dinner in the first place.

"There is no help for it, I shall have to send a note to Pemberley," Elizabeth said, a hand on Kitty's feverish forehead.

"Nonsense," Mrs Fischer sniffed. "Kitty will do well enough here with me to care for her. Just a cold. You go on to dinner and have yourself a nice time. It would not do to rebuff the Family, after all."

"My sister is sick. I am hardly rebuffing them by staying to tend her rather than going to dinner."

Mrs Fischer's expression turned flinty. "I insist. You go. You are too young to be confined to a sick room, and for no reason. You must make the most of every social opportunity you have."

Elizabeth hardly thought a marriage proposal would be the result of dinner. But she understood why Mrs Fischer was so insistent. How could anyone marry her off if she never *went* anywhere? And of course no one knew of her history with Darcy.

She glanced down at her sleeping sister. An evening in Miss Darcy's company was far more appealing than sitting at Kitty's bedside, waiting for her to wake up.

Darcy would be present as well...

Elizabeth rose. "I suppose you are right. It is not as if Kitty has never had a cold. But I shan't linger."

"Of course not, dear," Mrs Fischer said. "But no need to rush, either."

Elizabeth nodded, slipping out of the room to go to her own and prepare for dinner. She had brought two dresses suitable for a potential dinner invitation and chose one. She preferred simple, classic lines with puffed sleeves. She partnered it with one of her mother's simple pearl necklaces and allowed Mrs Fischer's maid to arrange her hair.

She would never be a classic beauty, not with her dark hair and eyes and robust figure, but she thought herself handsome. She was not *silly,* and she would trade an elegant, dignified carriage over Lydia's feisty beauty any day. Jane. . .well, there were not many like Jane, with beauty, grace and gentleness of manner in one. Her sister should have been able to wed, not wound up a nanny for their aunt. Elizabeth endured a momentary pang of sadness, the kind of grief that occasionally rose up and seized her insides before she stuffed it away again.

There was no room to live life in a state of perpetual grief and regret. She would only grow bitter. Truly, she was fortunate. She had not yet been forced into homelessness, or into taking a position as a governess. Not yet. She still had. . .options.

Elizabeth rose, thanking the maid, restlessness driving her spirits. Restlessness and a hearty dose of distracting nervousness.

"I will walk," she told Mrs Fischer absently as she descended the stairs. "There is still some daylight, and it is not far." The walk from Longbourn to Netherfield was longer, after all, and she had made that trip on foot plenty of times in the past, and after sunset, too.

Mrs Fischer did not bother to argue. Elizabeth supposed she was nearly infamous for her walks by now and found she did not care one whit.

Perhaps she should have, though. While the weather had appeared as cooperative as it normally was this time of year—grey clouds present but an amiable grey, not the angry hue of an impending storm—just a handful of hours ago, they seemed to have in a matter of a half hour changed their mind. Now they looked put out, indeed, and Elizabeth picked up her pace, imagining she was about to get caught in a sudden storm.

She grit her teeth with a sigh. Well, it would not be the first time she was caught in weather. And certainly not the first time she had arrived for a dinner engagement either soaked or hem deep in mud.

At least her nature was constant.

"Oh, blast," she muttered, and ascended from a brisk walk to a near trot when thunder rumbled overhead.

It occurred to her suddenly, that Miss Darcy had said she would send a carriage.

"Oh, good heavens, Elizabeth," she muttered. "That

is what you get for being so scatterbrained." She had completely forgotten, falling into her habit of walking to soothe her nerves. The walk was not so far, perhaps an hour and a half. Nothing she was not accustomed to. "Better to keep going or turn back?"

Hmm. The storm might not last long, and the food was bound to be more interesting at Pemberley. She would continue forward and hope Miss Darcy still possessed a humorous frame of mind when Elizabeth showed up looking like a drowned cat.

Elizabeth smoothed a hand over her chignon. Hopefully it would not become a storm-tossed horror by the time she arrived at Pemberley.

Darcy could not delay the start of dinner any longer. After arriving and greeting Darcy and Georgiana, Lord Randolph promptly retreated to his room to change for dinner.

"Three days in a carriage," he said with a good-natured grimace. "I should have taken the horse, but I was expecting my parents to come along. They *do* send their regrets. My mother is just too ill for travel."

That was a blow. This dinner had been arranged weeks ago, Randolph needing his father's blessing for the announcement. But perhaps it was not entirely a disaster. It would give the young couple more time together and give Georgiana more time to brush off the graceful manners he knew she possessed in preparation for finally meeting Randolph's parents.

When Randolph entered the drawing room, Georgiana went to him immediately, Caroline drifting closer as well.

"We are short a gentlewoman," Georgiana said, smiling up at her betrothed. "My dear friend Elizabeth Bennet is in Lambton. I think you will adore her. She is so witty, but kind, not at all mocking like some ladies can be." Georgiana arched a brow at Caroline.

"What she is," Caroline said, "is late."

"Perhaps she was delayed by the weather," Randolph said. "Raining on and off all day, and the roads muddy. I thought we might get a few dry hours, but the skies laughed at me."

Darcy went to the window. He had not even the weather more than a cursory thought, entirely inured to it, but Randolph was right. It was already darkening, and the overcast skies promised rain. Well, more rain.

"Do you suppose she is still coming?" Caroline asked, voice deceptively languid. "I cannot imagine what state she will be in when she arrives, especially with her predilection for walking. Heavens—*do* you think she walked? We already know she has no prejudice against mud."

"That jest is becoming old," Georgiana said.

Darcy frowned. "I would have thought she would

take a carriage. Does the family she is visiting keep one?"

Georgiana exclaimed, a hand slapping her forehead. "The carriage! I told her I would send her the carriage, and I completely forgot!" She glanced at Randolph and blushed and it was clear, at least to Darcy, why she had been distracted.

But what was Elizabeth's excuse? Knowing her, she had indeed walked. Darcy turned from the window and the first pattering of raindrops on glass. "If she was expecting the carriage, and it did not come, she might have already set out on foot." Because of course she would not simply wait like any sensible woman. He knew it in his gut. No, she was far too independent minded to actually *wait*.

I am my family and my family is me, for good or ill. I could never be wife to a man who refused to accept us all.

"You must go now, Fitzwilliam," Georgiana urged. "She might be caught out in the rain if she did walk. She would be soaked, or perhaps turn her ankle."

Caroline sniffed, murmuring words highly likely to be uncomplimentary under her breath. Darcy was already heading to the hall. "I will go to her home first. If she is not there, I will search the common path for her."

"I will come," Randolph declared. "I would not have it said I sat back in warmth and comfort when a lady was in peril."

"I thank you for the offer," Darcy said gravely, "but I would be more comforted if a gentleman remained behind with the ladies in case Miss Elizabeth arrives while I am gone."

"Do hurry," Georgiana said. "If she catches a chill I will never forgive myself."

"Oh, but then she could stay the night," Caroline said sweetly. "Or even an entire week."

CHAPTER FIVE

Upon arriving at the home where Elizabeth was visiting, Mrs Fischer informed him that Miss Elizabeth had left on foot over an hour ago. Thunder growled overhead.

Darcy reentered his carriage, giving a terse instruction to the driver to head back toward Pemberley. He had not seen her along the main path when driving into Lambton. Mouth thinning, he glanced out of the window as lightning flashed overhead. Confound it. It seemed as if Elizabeth was always getting herself soaked when coming to visit.

When there was no sign on her on the main path, he had the driver turn and search along a different route, exhausting several options by which a carriage might make its way from Lambton to Pemberley.

On the last such trip, he jumped out and strode

towards the stables. In the last half hour the weather worsened, and it was now obvious the independent, addlebrained woman had taken one of the many winding footpaths. Either on purpose to enjoy the walk, or accidentally. It was easy for someone not wholly used to the forests surrounding his estates to become lost. Especially when their mind was already of an exploratory bent in the first place.

Before he set out on horseback, he did take a few precious moments to inform Georgiana of events.

"Do you think she is lost?" his sister asked, brow creased. "She must be. I do not think she would take her time when she knows she is expected."

His sister was correct. Elizabeth's manners were flawless. She would not linger on a walk especially after dark and in this weather, when she knew her presence was expected. She would come by the most direct route.

"The search would go faster if you had help," Lord Randolph said.

Darcy hesitated, now glad that the duke and duchess had not been able to come. He doubted they would have been impressed. The last thing he wanted was for their son to become lost or injured while searching in the dark in unfamiliar woods for Elizabeth. But his desire to see her safe overrode his concerns.

"Very well. I cannot wait, but Georgiana may help

organise a broader search party and if you would head that I would be grateful. George, stay *here*."

"There is no danger of *me* going," Caroline said in her languid voice. "So you need not worry on my account."

Hiding his worry behind irritation, Darcy set out on horseback, muttering curses as a light sprinkle of rain confirmed his fears. They were on a clock now. He had best locate her before the steady patter became a downpour. He plunged into the forest, determined to find Elizabeth and bring her to Pemberley.

"Lost," Elizabeth muttered, pausing to stare up through the forest canopy. "This is untenable."

Clouds covered the moon, the swiftness with which darkness had descended causing her to curse herself as a fool. Why had she thought a *walk* would be the thing, knowing the unpredictability of the weather and having an obvious sign that it could go bad at any moment? She had thought the path to Pemberley straightforward, and indeed it was. But not when one was having trouble seeing, and had most likely taken a wrong turn due to woolgathering.

She sighed and began to travel at an even faster clip as thunder mocked her overhead. All she had to do was head in the general direction of the manor and she would hit the main path again.

By a half hour later, she knew she had somehow become hopelessly lost. Elizabeth turned in a tight circle, lips pressed in dismay. Panic would be foolish. This was not the first time she had been caught out in the rain.

Really, though, she was getting too old for this.

But another half hour passed by, though it could have been longer. Her sense of passing time was all muddled. Elizabeth stumbled.

Perhaps Darcy would send someone for her. It might take a while before anyone decided she was actually missing, but eventually someone would come. And well, the worst-case scenario was that she would be spending the night out in the chilly elements. . .completely soaked. . .in the dark.

Her heart sank.

Fate was all too happy to oblige her inner prediction of doom because *of course*. Elizabeth shivered, miserable in the gradually strengthening onslaught of rain. It had begun as a deceptive trickle, as if trying to fool her that she had time to seek shelter. But now her gown was entirely soaked. She blinked as raindrops got in her eyes.

Darcy would give her a look when she arrived at his doorstep drenched like a nearly drowned kitten. Her chignon was melting down her neck. It was past help now.

Darcy's opinion soon became the least of her worries. At a certain point Elizabeth decided to stop walking—since the walking was more along the lines of stumbling in the dark. She settled under a tree, arms wrapped around herself and waited, ears straining in case she should hear the sound of shouts or an approaching horse. Then she began to shiver.

At the point she began to hear such noises, she was nearly convinced she was hallucinating. Cold wracked her body and she knew for certain the thin gown she wore was no protection at all from sickness. Protecting itself, her mind hunkered down and accepted the inevitable wait while night continued its inexorable journey, until she could gather a burst of energy to continue on. She grew so drowsy she could almost forget the cold and close her eyes.

Horse hooves, though. She could not be imagining things. She was miserable, and close to catatonic from the chill, but she was not mad. Elizabeth forced her limbs to rouse and pushed away from the tree, staggering towards the sounds. Her muscles burned, and she realised standing still had not been a good choice. She should have remained moving, even if in place. Fool, fool, fool.

"Elizabeth!"

No, she was not imagining that voice with its tone

of tightly controlled anger and concern, or the muffled thuds of a trotting horse. Out of the dimness a dark shadow suddenly loomed, and a flash of white that could be a man's cravat. She had the presence of mind to step to the side in case, waving her arms.

"Here! I'm here."

The black horse reared as its rider pulled it to a halt, and Darcy leaped down onto the muddy ground. Every bit as soaked, she observed dazedly, but his movements crisp and hurried.

"You daft woman!" he exclaimed. "Why did you not wait for the carriage?"

"I forgot." She was exhausted. Anger required energy, and she had none. Also, couldn't he see she was drenched?

"You *forgot*." He said something under his breath she was certain was impolite. "I am going to put you on the horse. We must find shelter."

"Is Pemberley far?" She shivered as hard hands wrapped around her waist, hoisting her like a sack of grain, nothing courteous in the touch. Her foot scrabbled for a stirrup and she grasped the saddle pommel to help pull herself up.

"Far enough," was the grim reply. "Elizabeth, do you know you have been walking for hours? They will send a search party soon."

"H—hours? Oh. . .dear." She slumped again, so heavy and tired.

"Stay awake," his voice cracked like a whip. "Elizabeth."

"I am awake," she snapped, teeth chattering.

The horse began to walk, Darcy leading it by the reins. "There are huts throughout these woods, and I keep them well stocked. We will take shelter until we are found or until first light."

Something troubled her about that plan, but her mind was groggy and could not quite work out the problem. She slipped into a half hypnotic state until he was pulling her down off the horse, urging her inside a shack big enough for two or three people.

"I am going to put the horse in the shed," Darcy said. "Stay inside."

Of *course* there was a shed for the horse. Darcy, if he had bothered to have such havens of shelter on his land, would not leave out the horses. She admitted to herself, reluctantly, as she felt her way around in the dark for somewhere to sit, that it was yet another sign of the seriousness with which he took his responsibilities. She had flung unkind words at him all those years ago. Unkind and not wholly deserved.

He entered moments later, ducking under the low threshold. The rain battered the hut and the drip of wild leaks pounded against the packed floor in several places.

"Miss Elizabeth?" The rigid courtesy had returned to his tone, the bright lash of his anger gone.

"I am well, thank you." Her voice was low, tired. "I fear I have made a fool of myself yet again."

He seemed to pause. Her eyes were adjusting to the increased darkness, and she could now make out his silhouette. "We will not speak of it again. I will start a fire. I have ordered all these huts outfitted in the exact same manner."

Curiosity stirred. "A guard against such a time as this? Clever."

It was. She watched his shadow move confidently towards a wall of the hut, crouch down, and reach out towards something. In moments a match was lit, flaring to life and casting Darcy's face into a brief glow.

"There is wood already stacked," he said, sounding satisfied.

She remembered her hunt for a chair and in the new light found one, dragging it towards the fireplace as close as was safe. She certainly did not desire to catch her hem on fire and compound her evening's series of mistakes.

"My sister will send a search party soon," he said, rising from his crouch and staring down at her.

"What?" she asked after he continued to stare at her for several moments.

"Do you think you should remove your gown?" The question was carefully even. "You are in danger of catching a chill. There should be blankets you can wrap in. I will turn my back, of course."

Elizabeth froze, and then shifted on her seat, uncomfortable. It was the sensible thing to do, though shocking. She cleared her throat. "Ah. . .do you think it best?"

He moved around the hut, returned with a thin brown blanket, dropping it in her lap, then moving as far from her as possible. She turned in the chair. He had indeed turned his back. Of course he was good to his word.

"I think in the circumstances. . .recall when your sister became ill. She recovered, but it was a close thing."

"Are you implying you do not care to have me as an extended guest at Pemberley?" Elizabeth stood, attempting to inject some lightness into the heavy atmosphere, and began the task of removing her gown.

"You would be welcome as long as you desired."

She paused, head tilting as she considered the timbre of his voice when he said those words, then continued removing her dress. It would be easy enough to imagine things that were not present in the intimate confines of the hut, and with Darcy cast in the role of her saviour. Soon she had draped the dress over the back of another chair to dry and wrapped in the blanket.

"I am as modest as possible," she said. "Come by the fire, Mr Darcy. We would not want *you* to catch a chill either."

CHAPTER SIX

"Georgiana was looking forward to having you at dinner," Darcy said after they had sat in the quiet for a time.

"I suppose she is very worried by now." Elizabeth sighed, suppressing a shiver she told herself had nothing to do with his deep, nearly sonorous voice. "I am a fool. This is the sort of prank I should expect from one of my younger sisters in the past. They would think it highly romantic—trapped in a hut in a rainstorm, awaiting a dashing rescue. I am supposed to be the sensible one."

He glanced at her. "I suppose even a wise woman is unwise on occasion."

"You are very gracious. And you demonstrate the patience of an older brother."

"Are you saying I possess no patience at all?"

Elizabeth laughed. The humour in his tone was an unexpected flash of warmth. "No, indeed. Let me rephrase. You are blessed with the patience of a *loving* older brother. You dared the rain to retrieve your sister's wayward guest and have done so with remarkably good cheer."

"I did not do it only for her."

The brief silence was not quite awkward, rather it was slightly weighted. "Well," Elizabeth replied lightly. "I benefit from your gallantry."

"Perhaps next time you will consent to wait for the carriage rather than walking to dinner in your evening gown and slippers."

Her brow arched in defiance of his subtly edged tone. "There will be a next time?"

"Of course. You are aware Miss Bingley is also my guest? Well, I would not miss your battle of wits for all the world."

"Miss Darcy mentioned a gentleman would be present tonight as well."

"Yes, Lord Randolph. If she mentioned him, she must have told you they are betrothed."

"She did. I gather I was invited to lend her moral support, rather than for the pleasure of my company." She gave an impish smile.

"I am certain she would have invited you regardless. Lord Randolph's parents were supposed to have arrived with him today to meet Georgiana, but they were delayed."

"Well, that is fortuitous, since I have ruined the evening. I would not have made a good impression at all."

"Nonsense."

Elizabeth laughed. "When I first came to dinner at Netherfield, I recall you were rather disapproving."

"Hmm."

"Did we not discuss the qualities of an accomplished woman? I was found wanting and therefore not an appropriate companion for your sister."

"You are teasing me, Miss Elizabeth. I do not recall *that* conversation at all. In fact, I believe I insisted in my approval of ladies who seek to hone their minds through reading. I deem you a more than suitable companion for Georgiana. She would find value in a more settled influence, especially since she will soon be a wife and after that, a mother."

"Settled? Ah. . .that is the polite way of saying 'on the shelf' and quite staid, thus unlikely to induce a vivacious young woman to less than respectable behaviour."

He glanced at her, expression mild. "I find it fascinating how you seem to enjoy telling me what my opinions of you must be. Most often, they are wrong."

Elizabeth blinked, staring at him, at a momentary

loss for words. His tone was as light as hers, but there was sharpness underneath.

"Please forgive me—you are correct. No person can ever claim to truly know another's mind."

His eyes glinted in the firelight. "You have borne up remarkably well under the circumstances."

Elizabeth inhaled, forcing herself to maintain her nonchalance. He was not referring to the storm, and their forced shelter in the hut. There was a quiet thread of sympathy in his even tone, though no pity.

"Yes, well, one does as one must."

"No, quite frequently one does not do what one must." His head tilted. "If I have not offered my condolences on the passing of your parents, please accept my apologies. There seemed no good time to offer them."

Her smile was a little strained, but natural enough. "It is nothing. Time marches by and it is inevitable one must lose one's parents."

"Your spirit seems undiminished. Many women may have bowed under the weight of bitterness. You are still the same Miss Elizabeth Bennet, however. Well...much the same."

"And do you find my sameness a comfort, Mr Darcy?"

"I do." He met her eyes, contemplative. "I almost wish you and Georgiana had been friends years ago, before. . .well. She has needed friends of a more sensible nature, who nonetheless possess her same spirit."

"And what spirit is that?"

"A love of life. Laughter. An inquisitive nature and indomitable will cloaked in grace."

He almost took her breath away with the matter-of-fact praise.

"It is a strange night, Mr Darcy. I refuse to allow your fancifulness to go to my head."

Something in his face implied a smile, though his lips remained still. "There. You once again demonstrate remarkably good sense."

Her brow inched its way up—she was certain he was blithely unaware of his own masculine condescension, no matter how kindly meant. Elizabeth let it go. It was to be expected, she supposed. She also allowed herself a small moment of warmth from his compliment before banishing the sensation.

"Younger sisters can be a blessing, or a trial," she said instead. "I often found mine exhausting."

Darcy rose to add another bunch of wrapped twigs to the fire. It seemed as if the incessant dripping of raindrops had lessened as well, though perhaps her mind was simply attempting to ignore the irritation.

"They were—are?—spirited young women," he said after reclaiming his seat.

"Lydia has wed, and Mary—" she faltered. There was no shame in Mary's situation, but she realised she did not quite want to admit to it. "Mary is settled as well, though we had no worry for her. It is just Kitty I am left to fuss over."

He glanced at her sidelong. "She seems to have mellowed, but I imagine she is yet quite. . .ah. . ."

Elizabeth smiled. "Indeed. Time, as you say, has smoothed some of the less unsettling edges."

"I believe Georgiana will send me to an early grave. In some ways, I believe Randolph encourages her."

"She is such a sweet young woman. I find her presence refreshing."

"She is not that much younger than yourself, Miss Elizabeth. You need not sound as if you are quite *that* advanced in years."

"You are so kind."

A quick flash of teeth in a rather boyish grin, before his face settled back into sombre lines. "It is my fault. I have indulged her, I suppose. A young woman without a mother, or the steadying influence of a father. . ."

"Yes," she said softly, throat closing. "Yes, I understand. At least I had Jane."

"An elder sister *would* have made a difference."

"You could always find a wife, Mr Darcy. Some frightfully well-behaved gorgon to rule over the sitting room with a steel hand gloved in satin."

Darcy stared into the fire contemplatively. "Do you know that is precisely the conclusion I have come to?"

He did not sound as if he was merely going along with her teasing. "Ah, well, I wish you luck in your search. I am uncertain where you will find a lady as accomplished as—"

"Miss Elizabeth. You enjoy needling me again."

"There is little else to entertain me at this time."

Darcy's head turned, his eyes pinning her with a peculiarly speculative look. "Tell me, how would you have dealt with Georgiana?"

She stared at him, nonplussed, then rallied herself to consider the question. "You must confide in me some small part of what concerns you."

His mouth thinned, and he hesitated. "Her London companions are women all of a certain age and reputation. Nothing scandalous," he hastened to add. "Simply. . .political. Unfortunately Lord Randolph's father is a duke who is full of his family's importance. He wishes a bride for his heir of a traditional temperament. He abhors scandal or gossip of any kind, and Georgiana courts both."

"I see." She did, somewhat. There were talks of ladies in London who hosted entertainments of an intellectual nature. Some even considered of radical persuasion. But a young woman of Georgiana's beauty, family, and rumored dowry should have no trouble, even with stuffy in laws. "Perhaps it is just a matter of her setting aside some of her more intellectual pursuits until after the wedding and focusing now on presenting herself as graciously as possible. Which will not be hard to do. I cannot imagine any father not being delighted with such a wife for his son. Does Lord Randolph care for her very much? Is it a love match? Forgive me if I am prying."

"Not at all. Yes, in fact they met in London at the reading of a book by a woman author. They are very well suited."

"If he is suited to Miss Darcy, then he has a strong mind and character and will stand up to his parents for the woman he loves. Or else he is not worthy of her."

"I agree wholeheartedly."

This was an odd conversation. Never had Darcy been so open, so unaffected. Yes, they had enjoyed debates in the past and towards the end of their acquaintance his manner toward her became nearly that of a friend. Absolutely correct in his behaviour, but with underlying flashes of humour when they spoke. He had begun to seek her out at social functions and allow glimpses of his rather sardonic, but less guarded, mind.

This was a new layer to him, however. He confided almost as if she were indeed an old friend, or perhaps a favoured cousin. A poor one, of course. But the mere act of confiding in her and asking her opinion indicated a certain level of respect. How times changed.

Elizabeth grinned to herself.

Darcy caught the expression. "What amuses you?"

"Oh. . .I was recalling one of Lydia's scrapes when she was young. It is a relief she is wed and no longer my responsibility, so I have more sympathy for you than you know. Though I must admit times are rather boring now."

"Well, there is plenty of excitement at Pemberley if you find yourself in need of a new younger sister to corral."

His tone was light, but Elizabeth was touched. He did not mean it, of course, but the fact he could jest about a matter so serious melted her heart just a little more. She was a foolish woman, and mustn't let the masculine approval go to her head.

But that a man of Darcy's situation and intelligence would even in play consider her a suitable companion for his beloved sister. . .

She leaned toward him slightly, not quite daring to reach out and touch the back of his hand. "I am certain all will be well. No man in love would allow his beloved to slip through his fingers."

He seemed to still, expression tightening, but then the moment was over. "Hmm. You are right, of course. Still, I would be happier if she had a female companion until she is wed."

What must it be like for a girl to grow up without mother or sisters? Elizabeth could not imagine, and sympathy stirred for Georgiana. Miss Darcy was a credit to her brother, however, as she was an amiable and well-bred girl and with only a man to guide her. She would have had governesses, of course, and perhaps paid companions. But like Darcy said, there was no substitute for the gentle influence of an aunt or elder sister, or mother.

"Enough about my domestic woes," he said. "Tell me about you, Miss Elizabeth."

"I? There is nothing much to tell."

"No adventures to confide?" There was something under his tone. "No suitors?"

Suitors were the last thing she wanted to think about. Elizabeth grimaced before she could help herself.

His eyes widened. "You must tell me what has caused that look."

t was the last conversation she desired to have with him. Especially now. Elizabeth stood, covering the abrupt movement by approaching the fire, distaste at the thought of marrying Mr Langston fueling her energy. She turned away, eyes closing. Darcy, drat him. By his mere presence, he reminded her of how desperate her situation had become. Her suitor could never hold a candle to Darcy's intelligence, grace, manners. The casual authority of his bearing.

Or how every time he deliberately met her eyes, her heart trilled in response.

"Forgive me if I disturbed you."

"No—no, I am not—" she turned back towards him and halted.

He stood a bare inch away. Her breath caught involuntarily. How could he affect her like this merely by standing close, looking down with a gleam in his eye. . .caused by the flicker of firelight, no doubt.

"Elizabeth," he said in a low, slow tone. "You are upset. Tell me what I have done."

"Do not be silly." She spoke more sharply than she intended.

"It was insensitive of me," he said after a long moment, "to inquire about suitors. I. . .sometimes think it unfair what happens to daughters when their fathers are lost and there are no provisions. Before her engagement, I worried for Georgiana, what might befall her should I depart."

Georgiana would be well taken care of, but Elizabeth was not bitter enough to make that acerbic little comment. He had not meant it like that, and it would have been unkind.

An internal barrier broke, a small one. Blame the night, blame an oncoming madness induced by the chill of the rain, blame the man in front of her who enchanted her with his intense, quiet scrutiny.

"I have a suitor. I do not love him, but I fear I must accept his offer. He is a respectable man. I am fortunate at my age and with my lack of fortune to have an offer at all."

A pause as he weighed her words. "What does your elder sister say you should do?"

Elizabeth stared at him, a little surprised. "She

wants me to be happy, but she is practical. She will not advise me either way, torn between the two."

"I. . .see."

"How would you advise Miss Darcy? If she were offered a chance to wed for security, even though there was no love?"

"If he was a good man?" Darcy's head tilted as if he were seriously considering her question. "I might advise her to wed him, and that love would grow in time. If he was a good man. I do not think I could bear to see her miserable, though, so. . .I am uncertain. I am pleased that there is genuine regard between she and Randolph."

Elizabeth smiled. "You are as helpful as Jane." She stared up at him, eyes wide to avoid shedding a single drop of moisture that had gathered. Foolish, she was foolish.

Darcy's hand rose, fingertips brushing the edge of her jaw before retreating. "Elizabeth. Forgive me."

Her breath was unsteady. "You have said that already. There is nothing to forgive."

His head lowered a fraction of an inch. "There is always something to forgive when a man makes a beautiful woman sad."

Every part of her body was frozen except her heart. Then she laughed lightly, drawing away with a crooked smile and a raised brow, deliberately injecting mischief into her voice and expression. She did not understand what he was doing or why, but she understood that perhaps any man might become carried away when alone with a woman in the intimacy of a stormy night. It was nature, after all.

"It is a good thing I am not a beautiful woman, then," she said, then waved her hand, dismissing any protest he might have made. She was not fishing for compliments—she was attempting to steer them away from a precipice they might both regret in the sanity of daylight. "In any case. . .is it wishful thinking or does it sound as if there is a break in the storm?"

He looked at her a moment, then inclined his head and exited the hut, returning seconds later, the rain not quite a whiplash behind him as he shut the door. "You may be right. I will rely on your judgment. If you desire to make a go of it and hope we find our way to Pemberley before it increases, I will yield. Or we can continue to await aid here."

Elizabeth pursed her lips. "It is still far too dark to see properly. At least if we are both soaked, that will lend credence to our account and stall any wagging tongues."

Darcy stiffened. "I am master of Pemberley. There will be no wagging tongues."

She hesitated. "If Lord Randolph's family is wary of gossip as you say. . ."

"There will be no wagging tongues."

He was adorable, and a little scary. Not just for the

flash of indignant certainty in his eyes, but also the thread of chill under his tone. A threat against whoever would dare dishonour the Darcy name, perhaps. A promise they would be dealt with. She would remember this glimpse of him.

"How close are we to morning, you think?" She sat again, suddenly exhausted. She would never forgive herself if her actions led to any difficulty in Georgiana's relationship. Or, even worse—but no, she would not even consider it. That was too ridiculous.

"Not as close as either of us would like. It feels as if hours have passed, but that is only a feeling."

She glanced up at him, smiling at his wry tone. "Well, at least the company is not entirely unbearable."

"No." He resumed his seat, once again the slightly distant but more friendly than she had a right to expect Darcy. "Well? Shall me make a mad dash of it?"

Elizabeth sighed. "No, not yet. It is prudent to wait until we have some light to see by. Otherwise we risk greater injury. My sister twisted her ankle in broad daylight on a clear path. I would never forgive myself if the horse stumbled, or if we courted some greater illness." She shivered.

"You need another blanket and. . ." he swore under his breath and rose. "There should be a pot in here for tea. I am a fool, and you are suffering for it. One moment, Miss Elizabeth."

She watched as he rummaged for a second blanket,

murmuring her thanks when he draped it over her shoulders and then turned to search for a tea pot. There was a jerk to his usually controlled movements, indicating concealed agitation. Warmth blossomed in her chest again. He really was a good man, and a good brother. Despite a certain brief. . .undertone. . .during that one moment, he treated her much as if she were a distant cousin. It would explain the nearly familiar flashes of warmth that would otherwise be uncharacteristic in a man of his reserve and honour. There was no way he saw her as a potential wife, and he was too honourable to look to her for a liaison. How else would he sort her in his mind if he had felt some small attraction? Just as he was doing now. As a kind of pseudo female relative, allowing him to take care of her without compromising his internal sense of honour.

How lucky Georgiana was. How lucky would be the woman he eventually married.

Darcy continued to fuss in a Darcy way, and eventually a rough mug of tea was pressed into her hand.

"No sugar," he said, "but it is hot."

She sipped, suppressing her wince. "Anything hot is a miracle. Thank you, and have a cup yourself, please. You are my guide home—I cannot have you catching ill. I cannot carry you."

Darcy laughed softly. "No, I imagine not. Very well."

There was a cot, and so eventually exhaustion and a growing inner chill met with a resigned sigh and drove her to shed another layer of propriety and lay down. Darcy continued to gaze into the fire, allowing her some dignity. She managed a doze, stirring a few hours later.

"How do you feel?" he asked, voice quiet.

The rain had let up by the sound of it and unless her sense of time had betrayed her, it no longer felt like deep night.

She began to speak, clearing her throat first, and then sneezed.

"Ah," he said. "That is not a good sign."

"Inevitable," she replied around another sneeze. Her throat felt scratchy, voice hoarse even to her ears.

Darcy rose and approached to crouch in front of her. His hand hovered over her forehead, then lay gently against her skin when she did not protest.

"I believe you have the beginning of a fever. Georgiana was susceptible to them when young."

He stood, staring down at her with a frown. "The rain is a mist and I would be happier if you were in a proper bed and attended by a physician. Remember Jane."

Jane had almost died before her fever broke during

those early days of their acquaintance with Darcy and the Bingleys.

"Though I am certain a search party would have been dispatched. We discussed it before I left." He hesitated. "I could leave you here, for no more than an hour, and go out to look for them."

She began to respond when a distant shout interrupted her words. Darcy turned. "I heard it as well."

Elizabeth pushed to her feet, glad his back was to her, and he did not see her sway. "Serendipitous timing, that. Perhaps I should dress."

"Yes. I will go out and lead them here." He paused. "Do you require assistance?"

She shook her head, smiling faintly, and locked her knees, speaking through the dizziness in her head. "I can manage, and you have no proper training as a lady's maid. Go, before we lose our chance at a rescue before dawn."

Darcy looked at her sharply, as if seeing through her attempt to sound normal. But really, what could he do other than facilitate their rescue?

"Lay down, Elizabeth. I will return soon."

She woke to a stream of daylight through an unfamiliar window, the bed beneath her back far too comfortable for the likes of orphaned spinster Elizabeth Bennet.

Had it all been a dream, her foolish walk through the forest, a mad dash to shelter in the arms of Fitzwilliam Darcy, and then a barely conscious ride to Pemberley as his men, carrying torches, lit the way back to the main paths?

With an understandably hazy recollection of being escorted to the suite and tucked into bed by a house-keeper, woken again by the presence of an older man leaning over her bedside, Elizabeth slowly pieced together the events of what she was coming to realise were several days. Had Mrs Fischer been at her bedside, and Georgiana as well? In the back of her mind Darcy stood off to the side, hands clasped behind his back, carefully distant while others were present, but once they were gone...

"Get well soon, Elizabeth," he, or her imagining of him, had whispered in her ear. "You will not succumb. I am not done with our duels."

She slid out of the bedcovers, feet pressing against a cold floor and stood, dizzy, but that was to be expected. A bath might be in order, however, and soon. Her stomach rumbled, and she added a meal to her list of priorities as she looked around the bedroom.

As she explored the tasteful yet elegant furnish-ings, the door opened. "Oh, my, you're awake!"

Elizabeth turned, facing the round-faced owner of

the cheerful aunty voice. "I am also afraid I have no idea how much time has passed since Mr Darcy and I were rescued."

The woman looked sympathetic. "It has been three days, dear. And now that you are on your feet, I will have a bath drawn and breakfast brought up. Unless you feel up to going downstairs? I am Mrs Reynolds, by and by. Mr Darcy's housekeeper."

"I suspected as such. A pleasure to make your acquaintance. I am Elizabeth Bennet."

"Dear me, I know all about you, my dear. Now you go climb back into bed and I will see to that bath and breakfast. I am certain the master will be wanting to have the physician look in on you again as well."

Elizabeth started to say that was not necessary—she winced from the thought of the expense Darcy must be incurring on her behalf—but Mrs Reynolds hustled out of the room.

A gentle whirl of activity followed. A maid assisted her in bathing and dressing for the morning, the clothing proving that Mrs Fischer had indeed been at Elizabeth's bedside. By the time she was done and a small meal was laid on the sitting-room table, beads of sweat dotted her forehead. Her hand trembled as she sat. Apparently she was not as well as she had felt upon rising.

She was glad Mrs Reynolds had declared Miss Elizabeth not well enough to join the family downstairs. A light tap on the door came just moments after Elizabeth revealed the contents of her tray, staring at enough food for two people. Miss Darcy slipped inside.

"Elizabeth! Mrs Reynolds told us you were not up to coming downstairs, but I could not bear the thought of you breakfasting alone. How do you feel, my dear?" She took a seat and began pouring tea.

Elizabeth smiled, albeit a trifle wanly. "I am afraid I will have to trespass on your hospitality another day. I cannot bear the thought of a carriage ride back home." Indeed, even the thought of that much effort exhausted her.

"Of course not! You will stay with us as long as you require. Forever, perhaps."

"I must beg for you to forgive me. I am afraid I ruined dinner with Lord Randolph."

"Oh, he was delighted to dash through the rain on a quest to rescue a lady in distress." Georgiana waved a hand and smiled mischievously. "My brother has barely left your side."

"Darcy?"

She gave Elizabeth a sidelong look, spreading jam and butter on a slice of toast. "Mmm. Darcy. My taciturn brother has been hovering like a mother hen the entire time."

"Oh—well I suppose he is accustomed to shouldering responsibility. . ." But even as her voice trailed off, she knew her explanation sounded ridiculous.

Darcy was not a silly man. Of course he knew he was not responsible for her illness, even if she had been wandering woods on her way to his home.

Georgiana sniffed. "I shall not say more or my brother will have my head. He can speak for himself. Truthfully, it will be nice to have female company other than Reynolds or Caroline for a change. She is so gloomy lately, not at all agreeable."

Elizabeth murmured something suitably noncommittal, sipping tea liberally laced with milk and sugar before biting into a slice of dry toast. Nothing rich for her, though the breakfast looked delicious.

They ate slowly, in companionable silence, Georgiana proving she did not require constant conversation to be at ease. Her affable quietness allowed Elizabeth to relax and not work as hard at pretending she felt completely well.

"You look as if you need a rest," Miss Darcy said when they were finished. She leaned forward, patting Elizabeth's hand before rising. "I know it is tempting to be up and about too soon, but I will send you a selection of books and I am certain Fitzwilliam will look in on you as well. Shall I return for tea?"

"That would be lovely," Elizabeth said, grateful to her for understanding that she was not up to company at this time. It was unlikely Elizabeth would read, either. As soon as she crawled back into the bed, she would be fast asleep.

CHAPTER EIGHT

Her health improved, but there must of course be a cloud in every silver lining. As soon as she was well enough to come to dinner, Elizabeth dressed and was escorted to the already gathered party.

Which included Caroline Bingley, and a gentleman who must be Lord Randolph.

"Miss Elizabeth!" Miss Bingley exclaimed. "I see you are much improved. How fortunate. We may now be delighted by your company. Do not be perturbed by your appearance, my dear—we all understand you have been ill."

Elizabeth smiled, jaw aching from the restraint of ignoring the dangling bait. She was hardly a vain woman, but for a moment a smidgen of discomfort wormed its way into her composure. Her skin had looked a trifle sallow, the shadows under her eyes pronounced. Her hair rather limp. But who would expect a convalescent to be an example of glowing health and beauty?

Drat Caroline Bingley.

"I am indeed fortunate," Elizabeth said instead. "I have recovered and so many do not in similar circumstances. My own sister Jane nearly died."

"Yes, Miss Bennet. I have not seen her in so long. Is she well?"

"Very well." It took everything in her to keep her voice even. Once, Jane had thought to marry Caroline's brother, but he had allowed his sisters to sway his opinion and that courtship had never progressed.

"I am gratified to hear so."

Elizabeth met Darcy's gaze. He had risen from his chair in the corner and approached. His silence, this time, she did not mistake as cold or distant. He met her gaze with veiled intensity, but in that single glance she understood he was not indifferent to her presence—and forgot none of their shared conversation.

There would be a time for them soon—a time for her to express her gratitude, of course.

"One is grateful Mr Darcy did not also fall ill from the necessity of having to rescue you," Caroline said. "Really, how *does* one become lost on such clearly defined paths?" She laughed lightly. "I do recall you are quite the adventurer, however."

"I? Not at all."

"We are all grateful my brother knows these woods so well," Georgiana said. "Miss Elizabeth could hardly be expected *not* to become lost! But come, Miss Elizabeth, allow me to introduce you to my Lord Randolph."

Elizabeth found Lord Randolph to be a man of cheerful disposition, reminding her somewhat of Mr Bingley. "I so wanted to be the dashing rescuer," Randolph exclaimed when conversation inevitably wound around to her adventure. "But Darcy beat me to it! I was hoping to convince Miss Darcy what a brave and gallant fellow I am."

The young woman smiled. "I need no convincing, Randolph. Though I daresay Miss Elizabeth is the brave one. How long were you alone in the dark woods before my brother found you?"

Elizabeth smiled at Georgiana. "Long enough. It was foolish of me, rather than brave. I forgot about your offer of a carriage and as I so love to walk—"

"Yes, we recall," Caroline interjected. "There is no walk you shall not conquer, no patch of mud your hems will disdain."

"I have always found that a strong, healthy constitution is the sign of a strong, healthy mind," Elizabeth said.

Darcy glanced between them, expression

inscrutable. "Now that we are all assembled, shall we in to dinner, ladies?"

Darcy escorted Miss Bingley in, while Miss Darcy took Lord Randolph's arm. Elizabeth followed, resigned to an unpleasant evening gracefully deflecting Caroline's barbs.

And she was not wrong to so resign herself.

"Are you sure you are back to feeling yourself again, Miss Elizabeth?" Caroline asked.

"Thank you for your concern. I had no more than a bad cold." Elizabeth smiled with feigned cheerfulness as soup was served.

The smile Caroline returned was so chilly Elizabeth swore she could almost see her frosty breath.

"You must have been quite ill to have stayed overnight in a tiny hut, even with a man as trustworthy as Darcy. I daresay mortification might have kept me outside, and I'd likely died. But we have different constitutions and levels of what we will endure." She slanted a look at Darcy. "There are those who would misconstrue the circumstances. I pray Mr Darcy can trust upon your discretion."

"I am certain I may," Darcy said, voice chilly.

Elizabeth worked to relax a jaw stiff from forcing herself to smile. The implication was clear. Caroline warned her against attempting to use the situation to her advantage. Elizabeth's fingers itched to slap the woman. Miss Bingley assumed the worst because that was likely what *she* would do—reward a man's gallantry with entrapment.

"I insisted Miss Elizabeth take shelter in the hut for her sake," he continued, giving Lord Randolph a brief glance. "There was no impropriety."

"Any gentleman worth his name would do the same," Lord Randolph declared. "It is our duty to protect gently bred ladies—even from the weather. If Miss Darcy were ever in such dire straits, I hope whoever rescued her was half so conscientious."

"Yes, of course," Caroline said. "We all know how attentive Darcy is to what he perceives is his duty. How dreadful it would have been if someone other than the search party had come upon them. Imagine what others might think or say."

Georgiana lifted her gaze to the ceiling briefly. "But it *was* our Darcy and so there will be no tiresome talk."

"Need we continue this subject?" Darcy asked tersely. "Lord Randolph surely has no desire to dissect such inconsequential matters."

He did not look at her. Elizabeth understood. The matter was best forgotten, and now that her health was clearly in no danger, he must be anxious to put the issue to rest. She was well aware that many might suggest she'd put herself in the situation willingly to force his hand. How dreadfully fragile a lady's reputation was.

"Miss Darcy, will you play for us after dinner?" Lord Randolph asked, his eyes bright with admiration.

"An excellent idea," Elizabeth said, her expression easing. "I yearn to hear you play."

A smile broke across Georgiana's lovely face. "If you think you can bear it."

Across the table, Darcy's gaze finally met Elizabeth's, and after a moment she looked away. She wanted to reassure him, but it was better to keep her distance—any action might be misconstrued. As the dinner wound down, she found Darcy glancing at her more often. Caroline must have noticed as well, for her eyes glimmered like ice and her smile hardened.

Elizabeth, rather than compete with a woman so sorely in need of validation of her own worth, settled into silence, maintaining a pleasant expression even though inside her chest her heart was sinking, sinking.

She could not help but feel something ill would come of all this.

Georgiana played flawlessly to an enthralled audience. After finishing two concertos and an allegro, she looked up, her gaze falling on Elizabeth. "Who shall sing with me now? Miss Elizabeth, you have a lovely voice."

Elizabeth shook her head. "Oh, no. I would sound like a croaking frog." Everyone laughed but Caroline and Darcy. Caroline sneered, while the expression around Darcy's eyes tightened.

"I have heard you sing, Miss Elizabeth," he said. "Some modesty is becoming in a lady, but excessive modesty smacks perilously of deception—or making fun of one's companions."

"Very well," Elizabeth said. Protesting any further would only make her seem gauche.

"Miss Bingley, would you turn the pages for us?" Georgiana asked. "You may sit next to me."

Caroline narrowed her eyes but could hardly refuse. "I suppose."

Elizabeth was surprised the woman was even this well behaved—then realised that with Lord Randolph present, of course Caroline Bingley would rein in her worst tendencies. If he, a duke's heir, was to be Georgiana's husband, she could not afford to alienate him.

Elizabeth chose something lively which would showcase her natural alto and took care to sing her best as a dig at Caroline. Normally she sang only to please herself, but there was something of performance in her air tonight. And also, her duty as a guest. She would not embarrass Darcy by being a country fool in front of his sister's fiancé.

Elizabeth glanced at Darcy. His gaze was fixed on her face and he did not bother to disguise his attention. As the feminine voices joined and sang, he eased back in his chair, unsmiling though intent. He was still Darcy, after all. But his eyes softened as they met Elizabeth's, a connection that seared deep in her chest and down her limbs. She managed to look away, and saw how tightly Caroline held the edges of the sheet music, her lips thin.

"Bravo," Lord Randolph exclaimed when they were done. "I have never seen a more pleasing trio of ladies at the pianoforte."

By the time the music ended, Elizabeth was tired, realising she was perhaps not as fully recovered as she had surmised. Georgiana suggested a card game as they ambled to the sitting room, but Elizabeth's head began to pound. She stood abruptly, needing a few moments quiet if she was to survive the rest of the evening.

"I need to fetch my shawl," she said, excusing herself, and crossed the hall to seek it out.

Blessed silence. Her growing headache began to ease as she stood alone in the room, eyes closed, and wrapped herself in the temporary solace of solitude.

"I knew my memory had not deceived me." Darcy's voice came from behind her. She turned. He stood near the threshold, hands clasped behind his back, dark form fine and still.

"I doubt much does."

A rare half-smile graced his lips. "You did not always think so."

"Ah. Well, your opinions may sometimes deceive you, but not your memory of them." Elizabeth spoke more sharply than she intended. Whatever game he was playing, she must halt this now. He took another step into the room.

"My memory did betray me in one thing. It was not until I saw you again that I—"

Elizabeth held up a hand, drawing in a breath gone slightly ragged. "Please stop."

Darcy did not respond, but instead noticed she reached for her shawl and moved toward her.

"Allow me." He placed it gently on her shoulders, his hand brushing against her warm skin. Her breath caught in her chest.

"May I speak?" he asked softly.

"Why? For sport? What good could come of it?"

"Whatever good you might allow, Elizabeth Bennet. You are a guest here. I claim no power over you."

She laughed, low and faintly bitter. "You speak of power, sir. Now I know for certain you toy with me. Is it some last vestige of wounded pride?"

"I see you are not ready to listen to me. Very well." He began to turn away, but not before she saw the flash in his eyes. A familiar stiff coldness. She could not bear it.

"Wait, Darcy, I—"

He paused, then turned back.

"You told me of Lord Randolph and Miss Darcy. I must do nothing to jeopardize her relationship with him. I fear. . .well, we both know how innocent things can become something not so innocent."

"I have said there were no improprieties. No one present will gainsay me."

"Don't be naïve. Any hint of scandal—"

"If he would turn from her so easily, he is not worthy of her." But he exhaled, looking weary. "Yes, I understand your caution, Miss Elizabeth. I share it. And yet I cannot help but want something for myself."

Standing this close to her, he was very tall. His eyes a fathomless blue. When he spoke of want, she could not think. He was so close, she felt his warm breath on her neck.

"And while you lay so ill in bed, I discovered something about myself. Two years ago I may have been capable of denying what I want, but I am not capable of that now."

She inhaled to steady herself. But Darcy's scent—leather, tobacco, a hint of soap—came to her and she wanted to shut her eyes and breathe him in.

He smelled wonderful.

She wished to surrender and sink into his arms. Would he catch her?

"Elizabeth," he said, and took another small step forward.

What was he doing? Anyone could walk in and see them.

She wanted to say something, to tell him they shouldn't stand so close with others nearby, but her feet were frozen to this spot.

"If you were capable of denying yourself, you would not be here in this room with me, staring at me with fine dark eyes that I suspect reveal far more than you might wish."

She closed those eyes, struggling with herself.

"Do not fear us," he said quietly. "I would cut off my hand before I offended you."

His words were such heady wine. A woman could read so much more meaning in them than he intended. For all his talk of wanting, he had yet to speak that one significant phrase.

So she refused to allow herself to dream. But. . .she could give herself this one moment. And then banish him from her heart forever because to hope would shatter her into a million pieces once it was time to leave. . .and he did, in fact, let her go.

A cool, strong hand cupped her cheek. "Elizabeth."

"Yes," she whispered.

CHAPTER NINE

hey understood each other perfectly. His lips met hers in a restrained caress. Darcy shifted closer, the tension in his body obvious to Elizabeth, whose back stiffened as her hands rested on his shoulders. At her touch, the smallest dam of his control broke and strong fingers seized her around the waist, the kiss deepening, deepening. Moments passed and her body went the way of her heart in a sweet, tormented ache.

"Elizabeth." His voice was husky, his breath warm on her skin. His hands flexed as if unwilling to release their hold. "Forgive me. I know you haven't been well."

I am now cured. Thankfully, she didn't say that aloud.

She opened her eyes. He was still there; this wasn't a dream.

Footsteps came from the other room, and Elizabeth jerked away. Darcy took a half step back and turned, so smooth and calm it was as if they hadn't just kissed. And just like that, his cloak of simmering heat was gone as if it had never existed. She did not know how he could do that; hide all his passion and turbulent emotion in the blink of an eye. Elizabeth struggled to stuff it all away, looking down at the ground to hide the expression in her eyes.

Caroline Bingley appeared. "There you are, Darcy! Always hiding. You are summoned for a card game."

"Tell my sister I am coming."

Caroline's gaze flicked coolly from Darcy to Elizabeth. "I shall. Unless you are engaged in a more compelling game here?"

Elizabeth glanced at Darcy, who gave Miss Bingley a withering look and did not respond.

Elizabeth pulled her shawl around her. "Thank you again for retrieving my shawl, Mr Darcy." She curtsied and left the room, Caroline's silent disdain nipping at her heels.

Elizabeth turned the corner of the corridor and exhaled, her legs trembling beneath her. She leaned against the wall, a fine trembling beginning now that she was not forced to be so ruthlessly composed.

He had kissed her.

And she'd kissed him back.

Her heart pounded in her chest, but she willed herself calm. He'd made no declaration. She knew nothing of his true heart. It may have been a result of too much claret and their renewed connection after her rescue. It was foolish to think his feelings for her had returned after so much time had passed since the terrible proposal at Hunsford. *I cannot marry a man who disdains my family.* Her words rang in her ears. Oh, she had been so stupid. Even as stupid as she'd said Lydia had been. Perhaps more. She should have married him, and once she was his wife she could have practiced patience as he came to if not love, at least understand and tolerate, her family.

But Elizabeth had never learned the art of retreating from a battle in order to win a war. It must always be all or nothing. Which was why she was still considering Mr Langston's proposal rather than accepting him as she should have. Because he was not her all.

Only one man was her all.

Elizabeth realised she had been leaning against the wall for some time, perhaps more than a quarter hour, and forced herself to walk back towards the drawing room.

As she approached, female voices rose from inside

the room. Caroline spoke. "Dear Miss Darcy, let Elizabeth Bennet be a lesson to you."

"What do you mean?"

Light, elegant, false laughter. "Do not hole up in a hunting hut with an eligible man and expect your reputation to remain unscathed."

Elizabeth heard an inhalation.

"Oh, I do not believe your *brother* is at fault," Caroline continued. "You must promise me to look after him. I know you like Miss Elizabeth, but you can never be too sure of such a one's motivations. Her situation is so dire, after all. We must protect Mr Darcy."

"She is from a respectable family," Georgiana protested, "and as kind a person I have ever met. You are simply mistaken, Miss Bingley."

"I know you think so, and your good nature does you so much credit. But her sister ran away with a *soldier.* And now it seems she is trying to trap Darcy with her convenient 'illness.' Darcy would never offer for her of his own accord—the Bennets are too low to be coupled with a member of his family, and she will be a laughingstock when others hear."

Elizabeth smiled grimly. Much did Caroline know. He had already offered for her of his own accord, but Elizabeth would remain silent on that account. She had nothing to prove to Miss Bingley, who believed she must be trying to trap Darcy. But Elizabeth could not bear it if Georgiana was persuaded to believe so as well

—and Miss Bingley was right. Elizabeth could hardly blame Georgiana for erring on the side of caution. So many women must throw themselves at Darcy's feet.

She blinked away hot, bitter tears. She couldn't face Darcy now. She couldn't face any of them. She moved down the hall, passing the drawing room, resolving to retire for the evening and leave first thing in the morning.

"Miss Elizabeth." She heard her name just as she was to disappear around the corner. Caroline's smooth, cool voice.

Blast.

She composed her expression and turned. "Miss Bingley."

"Whatever are you doing lurking in a darkened hall like some gothic character in a novel?" Her voice was deceptively light. "Come play cards. The gentlemen have left us ladies to our devices for a time."

"I am afraid I overestimated my health. I feel quite unwell and feel it prudent to retire early. Please convey my regrets to everyone."

Caroline nodded, eyes sharp, and Elizabeth continued on her way, gait not quite steady.

He sighed, realising too late it was louder than he intended.

"Oh, a plaintive sigh! For whom—or what—are you pining, Darcy?" Lord Randolph asked.

"You've been staring out the window for quarter of an hour," Georgiana added.

How was Elizabeth faring? Caroline had informed him that she had complained of a headache and retired to her room for the evening. Only he knew that they had shared a single, perfect kiss.

Was she avoiding him? Did she regret their kiss?

He was concerned about more than her health—he was afraid she would run back to her home before he had a chance to untangle his emotions and gather his courage. He could simply ask her to marry him. The trouble was, he was not certain she would accept. And if she did, he still was loath to feel forced to wed because of her situation. He hoped she was not upset that he'd kissed her. She had returned his kiss with all evidence of passion, her eyes bright, her lips pink and swollen. After the kiss, before they were interrupted, her eyes sparked with a warm light he'd come to recognise that she wore when she was pleased.

At that moment, he'd wanted to confess all—to open his mouth and tell her everything he'd felt when he'd proposed at Hunsford. In fact, his feelings had only increased since then. But he'd lost his nerve, and then Caroline entered and the moment was lost.

He clasped his hands behind his back, hoping he emanated calm instead of the brooding restlessness that coursed through him. He could not go up and check on her even in his sister's company, no matter how much he might wish to. He must wait, practice patience. She needed to regain her strength. He need not rush. Now that she had come back into his life, he had no intention of letting her fall away again.

But when he came down for breakfast the next morning, she was gone.

Upon returning early in the morning to Mrs Frasier's, Elizabeth found her sister in the dining room at breakfast, and was forced to explain the events of the previous few days.

Kitty stared at her with wide eyes. During the time Elizabeth had been away, her younger sister had recovered the use of her ankle, proving the sprain had been much less severe than thought.

"Why are you even here?" Kitty demanded. "If I had the excuse of poor health, I would stay at Pemberley until I was asked to leave—and they are too well bred to simply come out and say so. Why are you not still there trying to win Mr Darcy's hand?"

"Don't be ridiculous."

"He ruined you," Kitty insisted.

Elizabeth inhaled sharply. "He did no such thing, and if you repeat that accusation to anyone, I will never speak to you again." She leaned forward, hands clutching the edge of the table. "Do you understand? Promise me."

Kitty set her lips in a thin line. "You talk to me like I'm a child, Lizzy. But I think you're the child. If a wealthy gentleman spent the night alone with me in the woods, he would be marrying me come morning! What is the alternative? A shopkeeper? A position as a governess? Sometimes I think your head is in the clouds!"

Elizabeth stared at Kitty, shocked. It was rare Kitty spoke with such adult fervour. So rare, Elizabeth could not recall that last time she had.

"Well, that is the difference between you and me," Elizabeth said, recovering. "You would think nothing of repaying a man who saved your life with forcing him into an unwanted marriage."

Kitty snorted, rising from the table. "You're a silly girl. I would eat my bonnet if it is unwanted. I saw the way he looked at you. Be stubborn all you want, Lizzy, and pay the price for it. Pride and stubbornness, that will be your ruin."

Her sister stormed out of the dining room and Elizabeth sat there for a long time, fuming. She had returned at first light, knowing that to stay at Pemberley was to court disaster. She would never wish to force a man to wed her for the sake of honour. It was not in her nature. At least Mr Langston *wanted* to wed her. If Darcy had any honourable intentions, he would have offered for her as soon as she was well. He had had plenty of time to kiss her, after all!

But that evening at dinner, Elizabeth realised from the worried glances Mrs Frasier kept sending her, that perhaps she hadn't been hasty enough in leaving Pemberley.

Indeed, that evening when Mrs Frasier knocked on her bedroom door as she was brushing her hair for the evening, Elizabeth's dread was justified.

"Lizzy, you must know that when I was at Mrs Smith's today, she told me she overheard Mrs Hammond saying that her daughter overheard Kitty saying how Mr Darcy rescued her sister Lizzy from certain death in a storm. And how they were forced to take shelter overnight and almost died before a rescue party found them."

Elizabeth's vision went red with anger. Kitty had done the very thing Elizabeth had asked her not to do. She set down her brush and rushed out of her bedroom and into Kitty's.

"How could you!" Elizabeth exclaimed, hands curled into fists at her side. "You deliberately started rumours."

Kitty sniffed, not looking up from her book. "There were already rumours. I just helped you along the path to finally wedding Mr Darcy. And as soon as you are married, you may thank me by finding me a rich husband as well. I'm much prettier than you and have a more joyful disposition. It should not be too difficult with Darcy as my brother-in-law."

Elizabeth struggled to breathe. She slumped against the wall, stunned and grasping for anything to get some sense into Kitty's head. But it was too late. "You—he will never marry me. I would never *force* him to marry me. You don't know what you've done. It is not just me you have hurt, but Miss Darcy as well."

Mrs Frasier was standing in the threshold, giving the sisters a worried look. "It might not be as bad as that, dear. Miss Darcy is loved around here, no one would speak ill of her."

Elizabeth shook her head. It was no use. Giving an unrepentant Kitty one last fulminating look, she pushed off the wall and returned to her room, sinking onto the edge of the bed. Mrs Frasier followed her as far as the door.

"You look exhausted, Lizzy. Rest. I think in the morning things will not seem so dire."

Mrs Frasier talked her out of returning to Longbourn earlier than planned, so Elizabeth's next thought was simply to stay inside and enjoy her friend's company until talk died down. Elizabeth was merely visiting, after all. If no one saw her face, she would soon be an afterthought. And perhaps Mrs Frasier was right—what real harm could come to Georgiana? It was a particular kind of arrogance for Elizabeth to think that somehow she had the power to affect Miss Darcy's reputation, and thus her engagement. In fact, it was preposterous, a ridiculous stretch of credulity.

Cheered, she spent the next two days reading when a messenger from Pemberley dropped off a note. Opening it and reading the few lines, she discovered she was invited to a picnic. Three days of no rain had dried out the countryside enough to take advantage of the current sunshine. Miss Darcy begged her to come and bring Miss Kitty as well. She would not take no for an answer, and this time, wait for the carriage.

Elizabeth hesitated, especially because she did not want to either reward or encourage Kitty's duplicitous behaviour, but in the end dashed a quick reply accepting the invitation.

This time she did wait for the carriage, and when it pulled up on Pemberley grounds, Elizabeth allowed Kitty to tumble out first, exiting at a more sedate pace. And looked up into blue, blue eyes.

"Miss Elizabeth," Darcy said. "I am pleased you accepted my invitation."

CHAPTER TEN

His quiet greeting was unexpected. "I— your invitation?" She mentally kicked herself. It was his house, after all. "Of course."

His lips curved a little, grave blue eyes intent on her face. "I will not admit I stood over my sister and dictated the words, but suffice it to say I suspected that if I wrote you with my own hand, you would have found a graceful way to refuse."

He spoke, low and nearly intimate, though he stood at a correct distance, posture aloof. No one out of ear distance would think there was anything personal about their conversation.

They would have been wrong.

Darcy pitched his voice in a deliberate caress, as if attempting to use the timbre to stoke her inner fire, to coax her into his arms—at least mentally. It was seduction, both subtle and clever. This was a man who was fully aware the way to woo Elizabeth Bennet was through her mind.

"Come," he said, and glanced at Kitty, who with uncharacteristic discretion had sauntered away several feet, taking great pains to look all around her with admiration, as if she was not giving Darcy and her sister a few stolen seconds to converse, but merely awed by her surroundings.

Proving she was paying attention, Kitty returned. Darcy bowed. "I am delighted to see you have fully recovered from your injury, Miss Kitty."

Kitty flashed a winsome smile, batting her lashes. She was not above flirting, though good humour sparkled in her blue-grey eyes. "You had best stay close, Mr Darcy," she said in an arch tone. "I have a premonition I will require such assistance as you rendered me again."

Abruptly, Darcy smiled. Elizabeth blinked at the unexpected display of amusement. But then her sister *was* charming in her unabashed, shameless flirting.

"Though I suppose I should let my sister have her turn." She slanted a sly look at Elizabeth. "Somehow I think you might prefer that."

He escorted them to the picnic, chatting—well, Kitty mostly chatted, Darcy made a noncommittal noise here and there, a certain warmth to the timbre of his tone Elizabeth had not heard all those years ago at home. She dearly wished to ask him what had changed. He had been so disdainful of her younger sisters, his restrained horror at her mother's behaviour plain, at least, to Elizabeth. To Miss Bingley as well.

"Miss Elizabeth!" Georgiana cried, walking toward them with her arms held out. "I see you waited for the carriage this time."

Elizabeth laughed, returning Miss Darcy's broad smile. "We did, though the day is so lovely I nearly changed my mind. The forests beckon me. I cannot imagine what it would have been like to grow up here. I should have lost myself in the woods daily."

"We nearly did," Georgiana replied, giving Elizabeth a kiss on her cheek. She turned to greet Kitty.

"I understand the temptation," Darcy said quietly. "But I would ask that you allow me to accompany you if you go exploring. It is not always entirely safe."

"Oh, my brother is eternally worried about brigands in the woods!"

"Not just brigands," he retorted, "though that is worrisome enough."

"You may certainly escort *me*, Mr Darcy," Kitty said with an arch look at Elizabeth. "I for one have no desire to run afoul of brigands or bad weather. Though perhaps there is some fun in the bad weather, as my sister has discovered."

"*Kitty*," Elizabeth said.

Georgiana giggled, then turned as a gentleman

hailed her. It was Lord Randolph, who was introduced to Kitty. Elizabeth was relieved to see her sister did not flirt with him the way she did Darcy. As the afternoon passed, Elizabeth found herself having to revise her opinion of her younger sister.

Tables and chairs were set out, and games for the ladies to play. Elizabeth recognised a handful of local women, many of whom clustered around Caroline Bingley. She almost thought she would escape the afternoon without incident, when a woman finally brought up the subject Elizabeth most dreaded.

Darcy, Randolph, and the other gentleman present had detached themselves somewhat, deep in conversation right out of ear shot.

"Miss Elizabeth!" the gentlewoman said. "You must tell us all about your adventure the other night. It sounds so dreadful."

"There was no adventure," Elizabeth said. "Only rain, and afterwards a bad fever. My nose was horribly swollen and I could barely speak for coughing. I looked like a drowned rat and felt like one as well."

Kitty coughed. "Not so bad as all that, I imagine."

Elizabeth's mouth thinned. "It was, absolutely. I was very unpleasant to be around." There, let them stew on that. No one could link romance and images of a sallow, red nosed Elizabeth in their mind. Surely if they came to understand how ridiculous their imaginings were, the gossip would go no further.

Not so ridiculous, though, a small voice said in the back of her mind. *Remember how he looked at you in the firelight. Remember how you felt.*

"But Mr Darcy did rescue you from certain death from exposure," the woman insisted.

"He did, indeed," Kitty said. "He was out hours ahead of the search party, and they were not rescued until deep into the night."

Elizabeth glared at Kitty, then forced a smile on her face. "Not more than two hours, I think. We were back in time for dinner." She knew what her sister was doing. "Kitty, did you not tell everyone how gallant Mr Darcy was to rescue you when you turned your ankle in the woods?"

"Oh, it was a bruise, nothing more."

"That is Darcy, ever the storybook knight!" Lord Randolph called out.

The gentlemen had drifted back their way. Elizabeth glanced at Mr Darcy, then looked away after meeting his inscrutable gaze for a brief moment.

"The rain was a sheet of black that night," Randolph continued, sweeping an arm dramatically. Georgiana rolled her eyes, giving him a smile. "And more than once I despaired of reaching the fair lady swallowed by the ferocity of the storm. But as we traversed the forest. . ."

Elizabeth listened with a serene smile as Randolph embellished the tale shamelessly. In any other circumstance she would have enjoyed herself, laughing at his gift for oratory. But it was at his and Georgiana's own expense, the daft man.

She cast her gaze more than once at Darcy, increasingly desperate, but he said nothing. Did nothing. Simply stood there, aloof.

What was going on? They had all gone mad.

Elizabeth refused to speak to Kitty and left early the next morning to post letters to Charlotte. It seemed as if there was a conspiracy to blacken Mr Darcy's reputation and Georgiana's by association—and no one cared but her! It was as if they thought it a game. Darcy had been very clear regarding his worries that his sister not involve herself in any scandals that might cause Lord Randolph's father to withhold approval of the engagement.

She posted her letters, then spent some time browsing the shops and even purchased herself a pastry with a bit of her hoarded funds. Dwindling funds. She would have to make some decisions soon. Charlotte was right, Mr Langston could not be put off forever. It was either him, or a position as a governess or lady's companion.

Growing despondent, she entered the haberdashery to browse and perhaps cheer herself up with something small and pretty. New trim, perhaps. If she was to soon be either a wife or employed, then she need not hoard her funds so ruthlessly, after all.

Feeling a smidgen better after having justified the expense, she began browsing, engrossed enough in a determination to raise her spirits that she did not immediately register the feminine voices.

". . .came all the way from her home to throw herself at him."

Elizabeth stilled, her hand hovering over a selection of lace. She forced herself to continue moving, as if she was not now listening.

A patter of giggles, cold and disdainful. "I have never seen so shameless an attempt at social climbing. She is barely dressed in rags, and thinks to seduce him into offering for her with some sham ploy like losing herself in the woods."

She snapped up straight, fury overriding any sense of shame at being targeted in public. Elizabeth turned towards the voices, her gaze pinning a trio of women she recognised from the picnic.

Marching over, she felt some gratification as their voices fell silent, even as she furiously blinked away what she refused to admit were tears. Some small part of her attempted to take the reins of her temper, but she felt her patience shatter. It was too much, at least for this moment in time. The stress of Mr Langston's proposal, the constant worry over the fate of her unwed sisters. Knowing how precariously her future hung on the malice of a few thoughtless gentlewomen —and how Georgiana's future might be affected as well.

And there was her deep, inevitable, abiding regret over not marrying Darcy when she had had the chance.

"You should be ashamed of spreading such malicious gossip," Elizabeth snapped. "Perhaps if you were not so ill bred yourself, you would have a harder time believing such nonsense!"

She swept past their gaping faces towards the door.

But they did not let her leave with the last word. "You should return home, Miss Elizabeth! No one here will have anything to do with you. We see you for what you really are, a shameless gold digger."

Not bothering to reply, she wrenched the door open and stepped out, running headlong into a warm wall.

hen Darcy returned from his morning ride, he was informed that his sister and Miss Bingley had left on a shopping excursion to town.

"And Lord Randolph?" Darcy inquired. "Is he still nursing his hangover? I warned him not to play cards with George while drinking." They were both incorrigible, which he supposed was another sign of their suitability.

"Lord Randolph has asked not to be disturbed this morning," his butler replied. "I believe his valet prepared a special concoction for him."

"Ah." Darcy remembered such concoctions from his university days. He rarely drank so heavily anymore, however. Though the days after Elizabeth refused him had been. . .difficult.

"I am told," the butler added with some delicacy, "that Lord Randolph also received some correspondence which may not have entirely pleased him."

Darcy nodded, considering the news. The duke and duchess had not come to meet Georgiana because the duchess fell ill. But what if that was merely an excuse because they did not approve of the match? They had had plenty of time to investigate Georgiana and ferret out some of the irregularities in her background of the last two years.

He tightened his jaw. Randolph adored his sister, that was for certain. The man would have to either stand up for his fiancé or let her go. Any family should be lucky to have a Darcy bride. It was perhaps fortunate the duke and duchess had not come, however, as they avoided his brush of scandal with Elizabeth.

Darcy set those thoughts aside and considered his schedule for the remainder of the day. There were various matters to see to on the estate as usual, but perhaps he should ride into town and accompany the ladies. He might see Elizabeth, or persuade Georgiana to call on her so, naturally, Darcy might come along. No one could fault his concern with her wellbeing. Although undoubtedly Caroline's sharp tongue would find a way. But then Miss Bingley was a bit like a gnat who could be brushed away easily enough. Regardless, if his desire was to win Elizabeth over to accepting his proposal, he could not do so unless he actively contrived to spend more time in her company. She would not be in Lambton forever.

Lambton bustled with people in the cool sunshine. Darcy nodded greetings to gentlemen and shopkeepers who recognised him. After trotting down the main street, he dismounted and tied his horse, heading toward the shops he knew his sister and the gentle-women of her acquaintance preferred to patronise.

The haberdashery was his first stop, and he reached toward the door when it flew open on its hinges, a woman careening out.

He caught her as she collided with him, his hands around her shoulders. He would know Elizabeth Bennet anywhere, even though her head was down. When she looked up, startled, he saw the sheen of angry moisture in her eyes and stiffened.

"What happened?" Darcy eschewed greetings. Her obvious upset did away with pleasantries. "What has upset you?"

"Mr Darcy," she said, straightening and pulling away. Or attempting. His hands tightened—he did not want to let her go. What he wanted was to pull her into his arms and kiss away her distress and then find the culprits and destroy them. "Good afternoon."

He narrowed his eyes. Any other time the huski-ness of her tone would have sent a tendril of desire through him—and yes, even now, it did. But the huski-ness was not that of desire, and her eyes were not bright from passion. "Miss Elizabeth. What has upset you?"

She looked away. "It is nothing. I am fine."

"You are not fine." Her lower lip trembled, then firmed. A full, soft, pink lower lip, and for a moment he had to remember where he was, so strong was the need to taste her.

Elizabeth shook her head and made as if to move around him. Reluctantly, he finally released her. She was not his sister. He could not grab her in the street and drag her away and demand an explanation. But he angled his body, blocking her attempt to flee, and gestured, giving her a look he hoped conveyed the hopelessness of her attempt to dismiss him.

Elizabeth grimaced, but fell into step beside him. He did not go far, just enough to clear the haberdashery's doorway and give them space to talk.

"Now tell me," he demanded. "Was the shopkeeper discourteous?" Georgiana had never complained about the man's manner, but it wasn't beyond the realm of possibility.

"Nothing is the matter, Mr Darcy," she said, voice tight, and he watched as she visibly composed herself, settling her expression into smooth, pleasant lines.

"Do not prevaricate. You are nearly in tears. Something happened in that shop. If you will not tell me, I will investigate." He took a step toward the shop.

She inhaled. "Very well. It was nothing, just a few

unkind words from the local ladies, concerned that—" she stopped and Darcy watched her cheeks redden. She avoided his gaze. "Concerned."

He was not an idiot, he could deduce the gist of their so-called *concerns,* and what a group of uncharitable women might have said to her. Darcy was unsurprised by his surge of anger, but also knew there was nothing he could do about it. One could not call out women, after all.

"I see," he said. "I think a cup of tea is in order."

Elizabeth shook her head. "It would only make the gossip worse to be seen with you right now. You are very kind, Mr Darcy, but I—I can't."

He tried again and stepped closer, touching her shoulder, and gentled his voice. "My sister and Miss Bingley are also in town shopping. Perhaps we might find and join them."

She opened her mouth to reply when the shop door opened and a group of gentlewomen emerged, chatting and laughing. One saw him and said something to her companions, and they all looked his way, of course noticing how close he stood to Elizabeth.

He stared them down, memorising each face. Perhaps he could not call them out for upsetting Elizabeth, but there were other ways he could make his displeasure known.

"That is not helping," Elizabeth said dryly. The group of women turned away and hurried off. "In fact

—" she cut herself off and sighed. "Thank you for the invitation to tea, but I think I want to return home and rest. It's been a trying morning."

"Elizabeth—"

She stepped back, mouth firming. "No, Mr Darcy. There is nothing to be done."

There was nothing he could do unless he wanted to cause a scene, so he stood, impotent and furious, watching her hurry away. He would give her some time to compose herself so she did not feel hunted by him, and then he would follow her home and they would talk.

"Look, Darcy's come into town," Miss Bingley said when he finally found her and Georgiana strolling down the street. A servant trailed behind them, at least three large hat boxes balanced in his arms.

"Good God, George, what have you done?" Darcy asked, momentarily distracted. "Bought out another store?"

"Darcy! Yes, I may have over-purchased again, but Mr Wolk does the most cunning little bonnets, and I need them in different colours."

He knew her shopping habits well, and that stores tended to do cracking business when she was in town. "George, we need to talk."

She eyed him, perhaps hearing the tightness in his voice. "That sounds ominous. What is amiss?"

Darcy glanced around. "Not here."

He took them to a coffeehouse and ordered tea and pastries, and when they were seated, discussed what he had witnessed, naming the ladies involved.

Georgiana pursed her lips. "Those three are never very kind. They jump on any opportunity to spread gossip. I only invite them to balance out the numbers and because they can be amusing when not provoked by the scent of a scandal."

"There should *be* no scandal."

She rolled her eyes. "Because you say so, brother?"

"The talk will die down," Caroline said in her languid, indifferent drawl, "and will do you little harm, in any case. Simply refrain from being seen in Miss Elizabeth's company. Is she not returning home soon?"

"I do not know her plans. But I would like to call on her and assure myself she is well. Being accosted while shopping must have distressed her more than she would choose to reveal."

"Accosted!" Caroline laughed. "A little malicious teasing, but hardly an assault. And Miss Elizabeth is a sturdy sort of girl. I doubt she has suffered any lasting harm."

"We can call," Georgiana said, "if only to reassure her. Perhaps tomorrow morning would be best." She tilted her head, giving him an impish smile. "You know.

. .there is one solution to all of this if you are so concerned for her state of mind. Is it not time to make an offer?"

Caroline choked on her tea.

Darcy gave his sister a stiff look. Georgiana knew his feelings, but he had not wanted them flung out for all and sundry.

"Surely that is unnecessary," Caroline said, recovering. "It is the option of very *last* resort. Mr Darcy has hardly ruined the girl."

Georgiana waved a hand. "I like Miss Elizabeth. William, you must simply man up and seal the deal, before she returns to Longbourn. I heard some talk of a—"

"Shopkeeper," Caroline sneered. "Surely you want better for your brother than a woman a *shopkeeper* considers his equal."

Darcy remained impassive, knowing better than to bristle and encourage Caroline's hypocritical classism.

"You mean, better than a kind, intelligent, lovely woman who has never sought to harm a soul in her life, certainly not with sordid gossip? A woman who would help my brother manage the estate rather than spend all her time in London shopping?"

Darcy lifted a hand. "Ladies." He waited until their stiff postures relaxed. "There is no need to do battle. I will spend the afternoon quashing any further gossip, and in the morning we will call on

Elizabeth and assure her that all is well. I will speak with her."

His sister sighed. "William, you cannot simply intimidate the ladies into sealing their lips. There is really only one way—"

His mouth thinned, and she stopped talking. He could not propose to Elizabeth until he could tell her that all gossip had ceased. Otherwise, she might think she had no choice but to accept his offer to avoid ruin of her reputation, or any brush of scandal anointing Georgiana. So he would speak to the husbands and fathers of the ladies who had tormented Elizabeth, and put an end to all of this.

Darcy, Georgiana, Caroline, and Lord Randolph took the carriage to Mrs Frasier's home the next morning, Darcy beside himself with impatience. The plan was to cajole Elizabeth and Miss Kitty out for a bit of fishing and a light picnic lunch, just their small group and no one else. That Darcy felt the need for the presence of his family and friends around him to shore up his courage. . .well, no one but him need know. He had spent a productive day firmly chastising the women involved in spreading rumours—through their menfolk—and was confident all such behaviour would cease.

Lord Randolph sat opposite him next to Georgiana, and the two amused themselves with a heated debate over George's latest book. Darcy took the opportunity to brood since neither of them expected him to participate. He could not help feel that allowing Elizabeth a day to stew in her thoughts was a mistake, but at least he now had something concrete to offer her. He would explain her reputation was no longer at risk, and then when she accepted his word, would propose. She would not refuse. He told himself this repeatedly.

"After a few hours of reflection, she'll come to the conclusion on her own that it is all just a bit of nonsense and nothing to worry about," Georgiana had said. "And after the pains you have taken, she may be assured of that fact. Miss Elizabeth is nothing if not relentlessly practical and good-natured."

The carriage pulled up and he jumped out, Georgiana on his heels. "She is less likely to tell me no," his sister said cheerfully, sweeping past him. He followed slowly, coming to a halt as the front door opened and Mrs Frasier stared at them.

"Good morning!" Georgiana said, flashing a winsome smile. "We have come to persuade Miss Elizabeth and Miss Kitty to accompany us on an outing."

"Oh," Mrs Frasier said, seeming flustered. "Well, that is—" she sighed. "Lizzy left a note for you. You had better come in."

Georgiana bit her bottom lip, handing him the note. "She is not here."

That much was apparent. Darcy took it, read the few lines, and forced himself not to crumple it up and curse. He turned on his heel and strode out of the house, pausing after several feet to gather his bearings. He heard Georgiana speak to Mrs Frasier, then the door closed behind him as he stared up at the sky.

Dearest Miss Darcy,

I have been called home to Longbourn to help Mrs Collins with her daughter, who has recently caught ill. I think it best, in any case, since in my absence the gossip should cease. Renewing our acquaintance was a delight, and I hope we will see each other again. Please give Mr Darcy my deepest regards, and thank him again for his gallantry, and offer my apologies for causing any difficulty, no matter how slight.

Yours Truly,

Elizabeth Bennet

Darcy's thoughts churned.

She left without saying goodbye.

Nothing else changed in that moment. The warm sunlight shining on them didn't fade, the fresh breeze still blew, yet he felt as though all the colour had drained from his view.

As though he'd been struck.

He had not acted soon enough, and his inaction had cost him his bride.

Suddenly, his cravat choked him, and the sunlight was blinding. His mouth tasted of ash. He lowered his head and focused on his sister, mind made up. "I knew I should have followed her yesterday. I let her go once, I won't do it again."

His inaction would *not* cost him his bride.

Despite his intention to leave immediately, it seemed as if one problem or the next on the estate barred his way. It took Darcy three full days to finally leave Pemberley after Elizabeth.

"Georgiana," he said flatly. "I will be leaving Pemberley for Hertfordshire in the morning. I will tolerate no further delays. I do not know how long I will be gone, but I expect it may be at least a fortnight."

She sat on the edge of his desk. "You *are* going to ask Elizabeth to marry you."

Darcy nodded, his mouth tightening. "I am. And when we return and wed, we will discuss with whom we will socialise in the future." He leaned over and kissed her forehead. "If I do not see your young man before I leave, give him my best. When do his parents arrive?"

"We are still determining that. His mother is recovering from her illness still." She took his hand and squeezed. "Don't worry about me, William. Go bring your bride home."

"Are you certain this is the right course, Lizzy?" Charlotte asked.

They walked arm in arm, Annabelle skipping along ahead. She had not been ill, of course, that had merely been a polite excuse for Elizabeth to get away. When her mind was made up, she rarely delayed in implementing her plans. Kitty had been furious, and refused to speak to her on the trip home, leaving immediately to see friends in Meryton. Elizabeth did not care. Staying in Lambton any longer would have proved fruitless. The pleasure of the visit was no more when she could not even walk through town without fielding gossip. Normally she would shrug her shoulders and roll her eyes, but she found herself unable to draw on her usual good-natured insouciance when Darcy was involved.

It was better this way. Her heart would no longer be teased by his presence. She had made a clean break, and now it was time to move on with her life.

"I cannot marry him, Charlotte. I have tried to talk myself into it. He is a kind man, and would provide a modest lifestyle. I have said everything to myself that you say, but I cannot bring myself to accept Mr Langston."

"You are in love with Mr Darcy," Charlotte said softly. She watched her daughter, a distant fondness in her eyes. "At least I had not already given my heart to another man. But, Lizzy, you must know that after you wed and have children, your feelings will change in time."

"I know. I *know*. But I cannot."

Charlotte sighed. "Well, if your mind is made up, you should tell him sooner rather than later."

Elizabeth nodded. "I plan on going into town today. I will tell him then."

"And travel to London?"

"Yes." She had arrived home to another letter inviting her to come and interview at the agency. There were a handful of positions available that were suitable. "Not right away, though I believe they are expecting me before the month is out. There is no reason to delay, and every reason for some haste if I wish to have my choice of positions."

"Lizzy, you can live here at Longbourn."

Annabelle crouched down, eyeing something in the grass. She would miss this child. She would miss her home. "You know how I feel about Collins. About Longbourn now. About being the poor, spinster relation. Longbourn cannot support both Kitty and I, and my sister shows no inclination of finding a position. If I go, we delay the inevitable time when Collins informs her that she must marry soon or make her way in the world."

"Yes." Charlotte sounded sad. "If you ever change your mind, Lizzy, you can come home."

Elizabeth steeled herself for the disappointment in Mr Langston's face, and practiced in her head what words she would say to gently refuse him. She thought she knew him well enough that her refusal would not lead him to be abusive, but men were capable of hiding their darker natures until after a marriage.

She walked into town, and after speaking several minutes with Mr Langston, left his establishment feeling both lighter and heavier of spirits. Once the decision was made, one path closed, and now it was time to embark on a new. She stopped to return a book to the lending library, and perused the selections even though she knew it would be better not to take anything out if she was planning on leaving for

London soon. Though she supposed Kitty or Charlotte could always return the book for her if she forgot.

The act of browsing was just beginning to offer her some form of relaxation when Elizabeth registered a flurry of whispers. She glanced over at the ladies involved, frowning, and cut her visit short.

But the whispers became a pattern as she completed her errands, and by then end of the afternoon, Elizabeth realized that someone—and she suspected she knew who—had spread word of the events at Pemberley.

Her dear neighbor Caroline Bingley.

Elizabeth returned to Longbourn, upset and just as determined to begin a new life away from Meryton. Only a fresh start would do.

She left the next day.

"I beg your pardon?" Darcy heard the indignant chill in his voice deepen into a growl and reined in his temper.

It was a lesson he had learned very young. A man controls his impulses, his father told him. A man does not give way to anger or emotion.

His late father had never met Elizabeth Bennet. Or the insufferable little toad she had the misfortune of calling cousin.

He now recalled one of the many reasons he had been unable to avoid offending her in regard to his opinion of her family. He was older now, and understood better the consequences of allowing his speech to trot ahead of his brain, so he would not make the same mistake twice.

Though he was certain even a saint would be tried by Mr Collins.

"Perhaps Mrs Collins has a bit more information, good sir—er, Mr Darcy. Ah, hmm. Yes. One moment, I shall call for my wife."

The toad who was now master over Longbourn scurried out of the drawing room. Darcy closed his eyes, mouth thinning. He was alone, so he allowed himself the momentary weakness of expressing his inner agitation.

Elizabeth, Elizabeth, wherefore art thou Elizabeth. His mouth curved in a grim smile. He knew she thought she had had no choice but to leave Lambton. No reason to trust him, after all. He had hesitated too long. Not because he did not desire to wed her, but because he did not want to look into his wife's eyes and see her suspicion that he had only married her out of duty. He *knew* Elizabeth. If he had given in to the gossip mongering and offered his hand, she would have refused out of a matter of course. But, blast her, she had not even stayed in town long enough for him to tell her he had finally solved the problem.

The door opened and a woman he vaguely recalled entered. Serene eyes, unremarkable features.

"Mr Darcy," she said. "My husband tells me you desire to know the whereabouts of our cousin."

"Yes," he replied, voice clipped. "I have traveled at haste to speak with her."

"So my husband has informed me."

A modulated voice, he recalled—Miss Charlotte Lucas. No, Mrs Collins now, and mistress of Longbourn. He had approved of her friendship with Elizabeth, seeing further proof of Elizabeth's good sense and character in befriending a woman so modestly behaved in public. The exact opposite of her younger sisters.

"I do not believe Elizabeth thought you meant to come see her," Mrs Collins continued. "Did you write her? Perhaps if she was aware you were coming, she might not have left. You missed her by only a day."

He tried, and failed, not to read a subtle rebuke in her calm reply.

Darcy grit his teeth and forced himself to remain courteous. It was only his impatience, and the driving urge to *find* Elizabeth and drag her home—no, no. Offer himself on a silver platter and beg her forgiveness. He highly doubted she would respond well to any attempts at proverbial dragging, even if his darker instincts were urging him to hunt down the woman he considered his bride. It was an unfortunate peculiarity of his, that once his mind was made up on a course, he pursued it with single-minded focus. Last time, he had allowed his doubts about her family to prevent him from grasping what his heart truly desired. He had no such doubts now.

"Are you aware of the circumstances of her departure from Lambton?" he asked.

Her eyes measured him. "I am, yes." A pause. "You are here regarding the matter? There has been some difficulty in Meryton because of it."

He stared at her. "*What?*"

Mrs Collins sighed. "Miss Caroline Bingley is friends with a few ladies here in town, and she regularly corresponds with them when away from home. The content of her latest letters—"

He held up a hand. "I understand." Damn and *blast* Caroline. For a woman who was so against his marrying Elizabeth out of honour, she certainly seemed to be fanning the flames. She could not help herself, could she, in her unreasonable dislike of Elizabeth.

"Well, after only a short time home, Elizabeth concluded it would be impossible to remain at Longbourn. She left for London yesterday. Once she makes up her mind, she rarely delays to set on her course."

Darcy hated to ask the question, but he must. "Alone?"

Her small smile was both knowing and humourless. "Quite, Mr Darcy." Something flashed across her face.

His eyes narrowed. What was she withholding? "Where in London? Come, you must know there is no reason to delay me. My intentions are honourable."

"Your intentions usually are, Mr Darcy. Intent has never been the problem. Elizabeth travels to London to seek employment."

Darcy stared at her, aghast. The words made no sense. "Employment?"

She busied herself with calling for a maid to bring her a lap desk of writing supplies, and took a seat on the fussy little couch, writing out several lines with deliberation.

"She would be staying with her sister and aunt in London, a Mrs Gardiner, until she finds employment," she said finally, handing him the slip of paper. "She promised to write when she was settled in her new position."

Darcy bowed, offered his thanks, and took his leave, nodding curtly at Mr Collins, who hovered in the threshold, then scrambled after Darcy with invitations to stay for dinner. Darcy barely maintained civility in refusing, focused on one task.

Find Elizabeth. Reach her before she accepted blasted employment and left London, and it was too late to find her.

Elizabeth wondered if she would ever feel angry again.

There was power in anger, a kind of emotional fuel that this all encompassing numbness did not support. Anger banished the spectre of helplessness, even if in the banishing lay self-delusion.

And who most deserved her ire? Caroline Bingley, for her deliberately malicious tongue? The town gossips who spread those insinuations that damaged Elizabeth's reputation and punished a proud man for his noble deed?

Or should she be most angry with herself, for not marrying Mr Langston because she was in love with Fitzwilliam Darcy, a pointless endeavour of the heart.

The dreary London weather mocked her, reminding her of the reason she was now exiting an agency for impoverished gentlewomen seeking posts, rather than home at Longbourn. Elizabeth focused on her present circumstances. She could not stay with her aunt indefinitely, not when Jane was already sufficient help for the Gardiner household. Perhaps if Jane had a potential suitor. . .but she did not, beauty or no. At least Lydia was wed, and Mary happy enough in her own post as a widowed clergyman's nanny and governess. Kitty would have to settle as Annabelle's governess if she did not marry.

The same fate was about to befall Elizabeth. It

could be worse. She could be forced to take less genteel work. One also only had to open one's eyes and ears to the London streets to realise many, many young women survived by working in far less respectable positions.

Her mouth thinned as she walked. Raising her spirits by telling herself that at least she was not a prostitute was an ironic indication of her present straits.

If only she had not visited Pemberley. If only she had not lost herself in the woods. If only she had not fallen in love with Darcy all over again.

Someone bumped into her from behind, jolting Elizabeth out of the past. She caught herself before stumbling and resumed her brisk pace until she had made her way. . .home.

"Lizzy," Jane greeted her, anxiety under a normally smooth expression as Elizabeth entered the Gardiner home. "Is it good news?"

They retired to the drawing room for tea. Elizabeth sipped the hot liquid, warming her hands and insides.

"I interviewed with Lady Amelia Weatherstone. An old family in the country. They have three daughters of an age to come out soon, and the most recent governess took a chill and died."

Jane pressed her hand against her chest. "A tragedy. That poor woman. And now you. . .?"

"Yes. I will accept the position. It is more of a companion. The young ladies are out of the schoolroom, but require additional polish and a chaperone for their frequent trips to town. I believe there is also some concern regarding youthful high spirits. The mother is soon to hold a ball to give her daughters a bit of practice and perhaps find husbands before going to London. And, of course, once the Season begins. . ."

The wages were a little better than most, with room and board also provided. The estate was far enough from London and in the exact opposite direction both Longbourn and Pemberley so it was highly unlikely Elizabeth would ever come into contact with an old acquaintance.

"They will need a genteel chaperone," Jane finished. "I am happy for you, Lizzy. It is not ideal, but things have a way of turning out for the best. You never truly wished to wed. Perhaps this is the freedom you seek."

Jane was incorrect. She had desired to wed for love, for respect, for the sheer joy of challenging company. She had desired the experience of her heart racing and her mind spinning in anticipation. The indignant or amused boil of her blood when an elegant, deep voice spoke a few choice words, his subtle mockery concealed from everyone in the room but Elizabeth.

She had desired—

Another mental slap. Elizabeth fixed a pleasant smile on her face. "Yes, I am most fortunate and I believe I shall be content."

There was no other choice.

Jane studied her. "Yet I find I am not entirely convinced you will be happy. Tell me truly, if Mr Darcy were to show up right now and offer for you, would you tell him no?"

"Of course," Elizabeth said. The small lie would not damn her soul. She told it for Jane's comfort. There was no need for her sensitive sister to feel sadness on her behalf. Elizabeth would rather Jane spent her energy worrying about herself. "I am convinced I could never be happy as a man's wife, or else I would not have turned down Mr Langston."

Jane hesitated, then nodded slowly. "Very well, Lizzy. If you say so. I truly hope you will be content in your new life."

CHAPTER THIRTEEN

*D*arcy stared at the lovely golden-haired woman in front of him, her forehead creased in consternation.

"I am certain she will write to me once she is settled," Jane said, hands fluttering before they stilled, folding neatly onto her lap.

The fates were laughing at him. To hunt Elizabeth down, only to have missed her by a *day*.

But Jane Bennet would not meet his gaze.

"There cannot be so many agencies for impoverished ladies seeking employment," he said in a tight voice. "Surely you can recall which one." She claimed she did not know where Elizabeth was heading, citing a poor memory. He suspected that for her own reasons, she simply refused to tell him.

Her cheeks pinkened even further. "I know it must

seem as if I am deliberately protecting my sister, but I assure you, Mr Darcy, it is simply my poor memory. The children require so much attention—I find it difficult to recall details lately. It never occurred to me the need to memorise the name of her agency."

"Or of her employer."

"I am certain the name begins with an E. Lady Evelyn Whitestone or. . .perhaps Lady Anna Warston. The estate is a week's travel by carriage, and quite in the opposite direction of Longbourn, I do recall Lizzy was most pleased. . ." she trailed off.

"If you recall any details, you will inform me?" he asked.

She widened her eyes. Blue, innocent. . .false? "Of course! And as soon as she writes I will inform you."

He would not stand still waiting on this comedy of errors to come to a tragic conclusion. He would search London until he found that blasted agency. A week by carriage. . .she continued to slip through his fingers. But not forever, he vowed.

It took him four grueling days to discover the agency that had placed Elizabeth in her position, but they would not be bribed into revealing her location. Bribed, cajoled, or threatened. He returned to Jane Bennet, but she gave him nothing.

"You cannot brood forever," Richard said. His cousin had joined Darcy at his townhouse the previous day. "You have a man on the case. Be patient. Your lady will turn up."

Darcy stared into his glass of claret and bit back unkind words. Richard was correct. It was not like he was trying to find a needle in a haystack. The investigator had assured him that it would only be a matter of time. Elizabeth was alive, after all, and would have left some kind of trail. She was not truly missing.

"She is a companion in a peer's household," Darcy said. "There is no telling how she is being treated. She is a beautiful woman. What if she is importuned?"

Richard drained his glass. "From what I recall of how Miss Elizabeth handled de Bourgh, I believe she can handle herself."

Darcy looked up, glaring. "She thinks herself alone, and without support. Like any woman in her position, she may feel she has no choice but to accept an advance."

His cousin sobered. "It has not been so long, Darcy." Richard paused. "Come with me to the country. Lord Weatherstone is giving a ball for his daughters, who are coming out. You need something to distract you."

"Are you mad? I will wait here until Elizabeth is found."

"Send your man a note, he will know how to reach

you. Besides, this is a country estate about seven days' ride from London. Perhaps they, or their guests, are neighbours to the household Miss Elizabeth is placed in. Perhaps you may find some clue as to her whereabouts."

That convinced him. And it was better than sitting around drinking himself into a stupor, or dashing around London like a mad man looking for clues. "Very well."

"Excellent." Richard looked approving. "We'll leave in the morning."

They left, Darcy's impatience dogging his heels. The last leg of the journey they made on horseback, thoroughly tired of the carriage.

"I cannot believe I allowed you to talk me into this," Darcy said to Richard, not bothering to disguise the sour note in his voice.

"Remember, the purpose is to discover clues to your lady's whereabouts," Richard reminded him.

"It is a long shot at best. I should have stayed in London. Good God. I despise house parties, and balls especially."

"You will live," was the cheerful reply. "And you owed me, besides. If I do not attend my mother will make my life miserable. She is determined I find a wife. This way I can report to her my diligent efforts, without worrying any mamas will approach me, far too daunted by your off-putting demeanour."

"If in three days I do not find my beloved, I will leave you to your devices," Darcy said.

Richard glanced at him, sympathy and amusement in his gaze. "Fair enough, old son."

"I *will* find her. She is in England. She is mine and I will find her."

"For all you know, she has wed some country vicar by now, rescued from her life of drudgery by a respectable chap looking for a quiet gently bred wife."

Darcy stiffened. "You mock me."

Richard laughed. "You should see the look on your face. I am a terrible person, I know. Apologies, cousin."

Darcy said nothing.

"What if when you find her she does not want to come?" he asked, sobering. "She ran from you for a reason."

Darcy urged his horse into a gallop. One more word and he would have his cousin on the ground, fingers wrapped around Richard's throat.

***

She had not been naïve enough to truly believe Lady Weatherstone had hired a companion of Elizabeth's birth to teach the three daughters of the house 'polish.' After nearly two weeks in her new home, Elizabeth realised she was a glorified child minder.

The twins, about to enter their first Season, were as

wild in their way as their slightly younger sister. Wilier, certainly. Miss Olivia was determined to wed the richest, handsomest man possible and Elizabeth was half afraid of the lengths to which she would go to ensure she wed the man of her choice. Olivia's twin sister, Phoebe, was less determined to wed, which presented its own dilemma. That girl was as likely to deliberately ruin her chances as Olivia was to ruin herself chasing a lord.

"Where are the cakes?" Rose asked, a discontented expression on the thirteen-year-old girl's face.

"Lady Weatherstone has decided we shall fast from cakes until the ball," Elizabeth said. "It is important your sisters fit into their gowns."

Phoebe snorted. "Olivia is already as round as a cow, so Mama might as well let her eat cakes."

Olivia continued to sip her tea, taking a dainty nibble of a sandwich. "Tell me, dear sister, how do you plan on disguising the spots on your face during the ball?"

Phoebe flushed, chest rising as she inhaled in temper.

"Ladies," Elizabeth said, a subtle bite in her voice. It was too early, and she had no desire to spend the remainder of the day keeping the twins from each other's throats. Especially when Rose would simply take advantage of Elizabeth's distraction to scamper off into some new scrape. "We are finished here, I think.

Let us descend to the library and choose books for our walk."

The twins groaned, though Rose straightened in her seat, eyes bright.

"Books, books," Phoebe complained. "You have not yet convinced me why we must read so many books!"

"Because you are stupid and ill informed," Olivia said, "and no gentleman of worth desires to saddle himself with a vapid wife, no matter how plump her childbearing hips."

Elizabeth's mouth pursed. Outwardly she had perfected a stern, disapproving mien to hide the fact that inwardly she was chortling in a most unbecoming manner at the girls' comments. If she had ever thought herself acerbic as a girl coming up, these twins put her to shame.

"Yes, conversation is an important tool in any young lady's arsenal if you desire an intelligent husband," she said instead. "Though perhaps when we are among company we might refrain from insulting each other."

"Perhaps *you* will find a husband at the ball, Miss Elizabeth," Rose suggested.

Olivia sniffed. "Balls are not for companions, you silly child."

"Why not? Miss Elizabeth is a gentleman's daughter, and she is prettier than you. All she needs is a proper gown and no one shall even know she is our companion."

"Do not be silly, Rose," was the sharp reply.

Elizabeth's brow nearly arched. Olivia's brown eyes narrowed, her shoulders stiffening slightly. Was the young woman discomfited by the thought of competition? Elizabeth hid her amusement, again. It was sweet, in a way. Of course, she was far too old, and much too plainly spoken to ever attract a husband at her age and besides. . .amusement faded as her thought naturally turned to her one—perhaps two—near brushes with matrimony. Even were her Darcy in shining armour to magically appear, he would never wed a companion. She wondered if Georgiana was yet married, then banished the thoughts and rose.

"Shall we, ladies?"

Darcy dismounted, handing the reins over to a stable hand.

"Shall I show you to your room, sir?" the butler asked.

"No. I have been riding some time. I would like to stretch my legs. Are there gardens or walking paths?" The land here was not the haunting forests of Pemberley, he would not be able to lose himself in trees and shadow until his thoughts ceased haunting him. But he could at least walk and try to exhaust some of his rest-lessness.

"Of course, sir. I will show you."

Richard, wisely, said nothing. He would make Darcy's excuses to their hosts.

It was perhaps a bit untoward that he not first greet Lord Weatherstone, but he needed the mental fortification before presenting himself to a lady and her three marriageable daughters. He was in no mood for socialising, but make courteous conversation he must, as he searched for signs of Elizabeth.

The butler left him and Darcy wandered the manicured shrubs and charming pockets of flowerbeds. The mistress of the manor employed a gardening staff almost of an equal to his own. He eyed one or two locations where a beleaguered man might escape for a few quiet moments during a party.

He paused to inhale the scent of air warning of rain in the not too distant future when feminine voices broke the silence. They were distant yet, enough so he might make an escape if he chose, but as he stood and half listened, something niggled in the back of his mind.

Laughter, and the giggles of young women but interwoven with such music was a deep, somber timbre, rich with intermingled amusement and disapproval.

"Miss Olivia," a woman said, the hint of a reprimand in her tone. "Manners."

Darcy stilled. The reply was lost in the shrubs perhaps, and he realised the group was making its way through the maze of greenery, soon to come upon him.

"Oh, fie, Miss Elizabeth. How can I maintain good manners when I am forced to endure her silliness?"

His heart beat ferociously in his chest, the blood in his veins heating to scorching levels. It. . .could not be. Life was not so kind.

"Nonetheless, it is good practice."

Was this some cruel vagary of fate, or a gift? The voice wrapped around his spine, slithering lower, even as the pulse of his heart sped in response, urging him to move forward. But his feet betrayed him—or perhaps they were his saviour. He was not ready to see her again, rooted still in shock. Had spent countless evenings imagining how this meeting would go. He would sweep into her life, banish her protestations, and steal her away. She would collapse on his chest—tearless, but eyes wide and shining with relief—as he explained he had searched all of England in order to confess his love.

Darcy banished the fantasy as the rubbish it was. Elizabeth was more likely to stab him in the gut with her pointed words than collapse on his chest. She. . .did not sound downtrodden. The merriment in her tone, a fond exasperation, spoke to a level of contentment with her situation.

For the first time, doubt assailed him. Perhaps she had left because she truly desired it, and not because she was simply unaware of his intentions.

Irony that now he was so close to her, he was frozen. Richard would laugh and perhaps strangle him. He wanted to strangle himself.

Do not return home without her, Georgiana had said.

And he would not. Darcy took a step forward.

The feminine voices were just around a manicured shrub from him. He couldn't see them, but their voices grew louder.

"On the contrary, Miss Olivia. One should never allow..."

The young lady stopped suddenly as she appeared from behind the shrub, causing her companions to look abruptly at her and then to him.

Elizabeth froze—but she looked quite well, beautiful really—before him. Her cheeks had grown more rounded and pinker than they'd been when he'd last seen her. She was lovelier than he remembered.

"Miss Elizabeth," he said, voice deep and husky. He bowed.

When he straightened, he saw she was staring at him like he was a ghost.

"Who are you?" one of the young women demanded. A pretty girl just past the cusp of womanhood, a blush in her cheeks. Well dressed. She must be one of Elizabeth's charges.

He glanced at Elizabeth, who inhaled silently. "Miss Olivia Weatherstone, this is Mr Fitzwilliam Darcy, of Pemberley."

"Oh? Are you here for the ball?" Olivia inquired.

"I am," he said gravely. "I have come with my cousin, Colonel Fitzwilliam. Miss Elizabeth, I did not know I'd have the pleasure of seeing you here."

It was a lie. Her eyes narrowed, but she only said, as the ladies around her giggled, "And this is Miss Phoebe Weatherstone, and Miss Rose Weatherstone."

He nodded at each.

"Mr Darcy, a pleasure to meet you," Miss Phoebe said, sounding as if it was anything but. The younger girl just stared at him.

"Miss Elizabeth," he said softly, stepping forward.

But she flinched away and clasped her hands together. "Ladies, we should head back to the house."

She thought to flee him again. Darcy nearly lunged after her, but now was not the moment. Not with three pairs of inquisitive eyes on him. Eyes attached to wagging tongues, and he must still be discreet. Darcy inhaled and forced himself to remain still, giving them a distant, regal nod. Control. Patience. He was in her presence. She would not escape again, and he would have a chance to speak with her. To convince her of his love.

She would be his wife.

CHAPTER FOURTEEN

Elizabeth's heart pounded still, even though she had been sitting quietly with her charges in the sitting room for at least a quarter of an hour. The older girls perched on a loveseat examining silk fabric swatches while Rose paged through a book.

Darcy. He had come for her. It stretched the bounds of incredulity that he had not. Of all the house parties to attend, and he had chosen this one? She tried to warp her mind into funnels of twisted logic, but every way she looked at it pointed to the fact that Darcy must have deliberately followed her here.

She certainly hadn't expected to see him. She knew guests were arriving for the ball, but she'd almost thought him a figment of her imagination when he stood, tall and broad shouldered there in the gardens. A bit of sweat glistened in his hair and on his forehead, so she knew he was real and wasn't her mind playing tricks on her.

But he was here. Attending the ball. She'd hoped here at Ogden Hall, she'd be far enough away from London to avoid one day meeting him by chance. She had not taken into consideration meeting him be his choice.

She must speak to him. . .and yet she remained here, frozen.

Rose was gazing at her curiously again. Elizabeth forced her brow to smooth cheerfully, hoping she looked convincing.

"Didn't I tell you we would find a clue?" Richard laughed uproariously before throwing back his glass of brandy.

Darcy's irritation increased considerably. "She is here, Richard. But I must still wait to speak with her. There are enough guests of the ton here that if I cause a scandal, then Lord Randolph's parents may get a whiff of it. And I would prefer no one know she was once a companion."

"Ah, your snobbery is showing there, cousin."

"I do not care for myself. But it would make things difficult for her when she socialises. Society can be cruel enough without such a thing as provocation."

"Eh. She would not be the first impoverished gentlewoman turned lady's companion to marry well." Richard shrugged. "You are overthinking as usual. Be discreet if you must, but don't be a stick in the mud." Richard set down his crystal glass, still chuckling. "I cannot wait to see Lady Catherine's face when she hears of this. Promise me you'll let me be present when you tell her."

Darcy scowled, stood abruptly, and walked to the fireplace.

Richard only laughed harder. "The irony! Perfect Darcy marries the help." He wiped at an eye as though he'd produced tears while laughing.

"She is the daughter of a gentleman," Darcy snapped.

"You know I don't care if you marry the scullery maid. Other family members may have a different reaction."

"Don't you think I am aware of how our family will respond? Do you think I'm a fool?"

Richard sighed. "We'll figure something out. Haven't we always gotten out of any real trouble in our lives?" He poured himself, and Darcy, another slug of brandy. "Here, drink this."

Darcy turned to his cousin, his eyes glimmering in the firelight. "This isn't one of our schoolboy scrapes. This woman is. . ." he paused as though he were searching for the right word, *"everything.* I lost her once. I cannot risk it again."

Richard threw back his brandy and stared thoughtfully into his glass. "I know, true love and all that."

Miss Olivia ignored her sisters and turned her attention to their governess, the lovely Miss Elizabeth, who sat near a window with a book in her lap.

There was something about her that Olivia couldn't place.

Not in her manners or carriage, both of which were unfailing. In fact, she was remarkably clever and lovely. No governess she'd observed had been both as pretty and as charming as Miss Elizabeth. She'd encountered ones that were handsome—to be sure, and clever and educated, but even then, there was an almost imperceptible quality that set them apart from ladies in society. A smoothness that made her both confident and yet still interested and kind in conversation. She not only spoke well, she listened and made the speaker feel important, no matter whether it was the gardener or her own mama. Maybe her grace was a quality that one inherited in the blood, as her mama always claimed.

It was a quality Miss Elizabeth had in spades. Which her mother didn't fail to constantly point out.

Olivia was thoroughly sick of being compared to Miss Elizabeth and coming up short.

"Miss Olivia, it is poor form to stare at someone. Is there something on your mind?" Miss Elizabeth asked.

Phoebe snatched the ribbon from the table in front of them. Olivia stood. "Phoebe, give me back the ribbon!"

Elizabeth set down her book. "Girls. Surely there is another ribbon."

"This is the one I want for the ball," Olivia replied coldly.

"Miss Elizabeth, do *you* enjoy dancing?" Rose asked.

Elizabeth smiled faintly. "Dancing is one the singular joys in life, I believe."

Rose smiled. "Then you should attend the ball."

"The ball is for guests, not servants," Phoebe said.

"She is a gentleman's daughter, you know," Rose said.

"Mama would never allow it."

"Rightly so." Elizabeth attempted to rein in the conversation. "The ball is not the place for me. But I will help you prepare. And then I will be very happy to sit with a good book while you all dance."

Phoebe rolled her green eyes. "God, how boring."

Elizabeth smiled kindly. "Not at all. I'm quite looking forward to it."

For a moment Olivia felt a small satisfaction that

the paragon Miss Elizabeth would have to attend the ball as a servant, and not a guest, and would not be competition for any of the gentlemen. At least she would not have to endure her mother's ire at the end of the ball that Miss Elizabeth had outshone Olivia in every way.

The library was cool and quiet, which was at least partially why Elizabeth liked it.

But also, books. She deeply inhaled the pulpy scent of old pages, a smell she'd grown to love and still associated with her father's office.

Fortunately, no one else was present.

She'd taken dinner alone in her room, so she wouldn't have to engage in conversation with guests, particularly Darcy. Lady Weatherstone agreed it best that Elizabeth sup on her own. Now that dinner was over and the guests gathered downstairs for cards, she could choose a tome with which to retire for the evening.

The books beckoned to her, and she moved closer, admiring their straight, tidy spines. She reached up and ran her fingers along the raised gilt edges of the spines.

A noise. She stopped.

A male cleared his throat behind her.

She turned, meeting Darcy's stormy blue eyes.

"I'm sorry to startle you, Elizabeth. I wished to speak with you, but you weren't present at dinner. So I had to come and find you."

A pang clutched her heart. Seeing him unexpectedly still made her gasp.

"Lady Weatherstone gave me leave to sup alone in my room," she said, managing to sound normal.

Was it possible he did not know she was a servant here? It struck her suddenly, that perhaps he had followed her thinking she was a guest. Surely he would not lower himself to make an offer to a servant?

Another thought occurred to her, a darker thought.

Now that you are a servant, he need not offer for you at all. At least not offer marriage.

Elizabeth inhaled abruptly, struggling to banish that thought. He could not, he *would* not.

She made a sudden noise in the back of her throat and moved past him to flee.

Strong hands grasped her arms, bringing her to a halt before she was even two steps beyond him.

"No," he said in her ear, voice steely. "Not again. Never again. You must listen to me, Elizabeth."

He pulled her back against his chest, his arms wrapping around her in an embrace that was a cage. She closed her eyes.

"I cannot be here alone with you," she said, voice

trembling. "Darcy, you must let me go. I can't be what you want me to be."

"You have no idea what I want." His voice in her ear, his lips on the curve of her lobe. She gasped, desire wracking a shiver through her body. He turned her in his arms, fingers under her chin, forcing her to look up. "You left Pemberley before I had a chance to speak." His voice was dark, his eyes darker. Pressed against him like this, Elizabeth blushed, the evidence of his passion clear.

"I don't understand," she said.

Darcy lowered his head, his lips hovering over hers. "Why did you leave Pemberley so suddenly?"

"I. . .I thought it best." Was he really asking her to explain?

"The next time you think something 'best,' pray discuss it with me first. You could have saved us both a great deal of travel."

He seized her mouth, his lips pressing down on hers in a kiss that was as ferocious as it was restrained. His hands flexed around her waist, but did not stray. Tension hummed through his body, and after a moment he tore away, covering his eyes for a moment.

Tears pricked behind her eyes. She couldn't speak.

He lowered his hand and when he saw her distress, his eyes softened. "I take responsibility. I should have made what I wanted plain from the beginning."

For God's sake, was he about to offer to make her

his mistress?

"Please stop," she said, averting her gaze. "I said I cannot be what you want."

He was silent for a long moment, but she knew better than to try to escape before he let her go. No, she had to hear from his lips that he understood her refusal.

"I don't think you know what I want, Elizabeth. . ." he said in a slow drawl. "And I am almost angry enough with you to allow you to continue thinking what I suspect you are thinking."

"What?" His statement threw her off. It made no sense, unless. . .

"Elizabeth. The idea of you is always with me. It finds its way into my very being. I cannot look at something and not think 'That may please Elizabeth' or 'Would she enjoy this?' It is as though. . ." he paused. "It is as though a part of you has entered my heart. I thought once I might move past those thoughts, but I see now that was in vain."

She closed her eyes as a tear slid down one of her cheeks. His words were exactly what she wanted to hear. He would not toy with her so, if being his mistress was his intent.

Footsteps rose outside the door. Then Colonel Fitzwilliam's voice. "Darcy, where have you gone? We are playing cards, and I need you to play so that I can win some of your money."

Darcy's mouth thinned. "We must continue this conversation. It is always thus with you and I. One impediment or another." His eyes flashed with anger.

She nodded, and he raised her hand and pressed it to his lips.

"My Elizabeth," he said softly. "Please do not run away again. As you see, I will only follow you."

She bit her lip and smiled. "I've run out of governess positions to take."

His expression darkened, but the library door opened the, and Darcy released her hand. Colonel Fitzwilliam poked his head inside. "Ah, there you are. . ." He saw Elizabeth and stepped back. "Pardon me, madam. Cousin, I have been sent to fetch you."

"You should take your leave," Elizabeth said.

Darcy nodded, his eyes holding hers a moment longer, and her own lips turned upwards in response.

He bowed and after a moment, she was alone in the quiet room again. She grasped the first book she saw and willed her shaky legs to walk back to her room.

Lady Weatherstone, hidden behind a bookshelf, watched Elizabeth leave.

CHAPTER FIFTEEN

*E*lizabeth woke up the next morning—after she had finally fallen asleep—still uncertain her conversation with Darcy hadn't been a dream. A wonderful dream. But, no, the book she had taken from the library (she had not read a word of it) lay on the bedside table next to a candle, proof that the kiss, and his words, had indeed occurred.

But uncertainty still churned in her as she joined her charges in the breakfast room. He had not said the magic words, and they had not discussed the. . .logistics. She was still uncomfortable with the thought of inadvertently bringing scandal to his family name, and there was the matter of Georgiana. Elizabeth knew she would not refuse Darcy a second time, but their betrothal must be handled with discretion.

And first there was a ball to get her young ladies

through. Elizabeth would discharge that part of her duty first. Only a few more days, and then she could finally have her heart's desire.

"I am inexplicably tired," Phoebe said, slipping into her chair and stifling a yawn. Elizabeth knew the girls had stayed up late playing cards with the other guests because she heard them come in late after she'd gone to bed.

"You were up till almost one in the morning," Olivia said. "It's not inexplicable, you ninny. It's completely explicable. You stayed up too late."

Phoebe pouted as coffee was poured into her cup. "La, I went to bed not ten minutes after you. I feel quite bedraggled."

The door opened and Lady Weatherstone entered. Her gaze swept over her three daughters. "You both look as though a barn cat dragged you in," she said to her two eldest. "Miss Elizabeth, do remind my daughters of the importance of beauty sleep to look fresh."

"Of course, ma'am," Elizabeth said, smiling at the girls. "Although I do think an occasional late night with good company is sometimes worth the fatigue. And they are so young and lovely, one can hardly tell."

Lady Weatherstone's gaze chilled her. "I wish them to look as fresh as possible for the ball. Rose, sit up straight."

Next to her, Rose straightened and Elizabeth reminded herself of Lady Weatherstone's instructions earlier that week. She was charged with helping the girls navigate the ball and find husbands, not helping them enjoy themselves. She sighed to herself. Every home she wound up in, the problems were the same. The problems of making a suitable match.

"I am not having any more than coffee this morning," Phoebe said. "My dress is tight enough."

Olivia snorted. "It's a bit late for that concern."

Elizabeth frowned. She'd always thought that starving oneself the day of a party was a silly idea. "But you will need your strength for a long day. At least have some fruit or eggs. Neither is heavy in the stomach."

"Melon only. You know strawberries give you blotches," Lady Weatherstone warned.

"Mother, do not vex me this morning. I am already cross."

Elizabeth sipped her tea and said nothing. She wondered what Darcy was doing this morning. Certainly having a better time than she.

"Tell me, girls," Lady Weatherstone said, "have any of the gentlemen caught your eye?"

Phoebe gave Olivia a sideways glance and smirked. "There is one whose eyes is caught. Colonel Fitzwilliam cannot take his gaze away from Olivia."

Lady Weatherstone raised a brow. "Interesting."

Olivia's eyes flashed. "He laughs at me with his eyes."

Phoebe snorted. "Eyes do not laugh, you silly girl. *I* like him."

"Well, I do not, even if he is handsome." Olivia blushed.

"You're just afraid you won't be able to wrap him around your finger."

"All men can be wrapped around one's finger if you study them right," Lady Weatherstone said. Olivia said nothing. "Miss Elizabeth," Lady Weatherstone turned to her with a cool look. "How was your evening last night?"

Elizabeth was surprised. "Uneventful. I chose a book from the library."

"Yes. . .the library. And what are you currently reading?"

Elizabeth had completely forgotten which book she had taken because she hadn't read any of it. "Robinson Crusoe." She was not enjoying her employer's new attention.

"I read that last year," Miss Rose said, and Elizabeth tried to smile at her.

"Lord, more books," Olivia said and rolled her eyes. "Mother, why do you care what book Miss Elizabeth reads?"

Lady Weatherstone sipped her coffee with a chilly smile. "You could do with a bit more time spent reading, Olivia. Men may pretend they like silly women, but no ignorant miss can be a successful hostess."

Elizabeth forced her lips into a smile she did not feel and shook her head. "It was quite dull, I'm afraid."

"Dull, indeed," Lady Weatherstone repeated, her gaze drilling into Elizabeth's.

"Well, I won three hands of loo and ten pence from Mr Darcy," Olivia said. "You should have seen his face!"

"No one cares," Phoebe muttered. Olivia was about to retort, but intercepted her mother's faint glare.

Mention of Darcy sent a bolt of adrenaline through Elizabeth. She chided herself for her reaction. Of course he returned to the guests and played cards last night. She shouldn't be surprised. But a queasy sensation formed in her chest.

"Mr Darcy, you say? He is a handsome young man," Lady Weatherstone said. "What do you think, Miss Elizabeth? Is he a suitable match for my Olivia? Come, what do you know of him?"

"No more that you, I would say," Elizabeth said. "I understand he comes from a wealthy family with a grand estate. And he is certainly handsome. I see no reason why he would not be a suitable match for any lady."

"Indeed," Olivia said. "I find him a trifle cold. However, I could warm myself well enough as the mistress of a grand estate."

Lady Weatherstone pursed her lips. "Ah, Pemberley, I recall. Yes, a grand estate indeed. There was some talk of ten thousand pounds a year."

"Quite," Elizabeth murmured.

"We shall endeavour to put you in his path, Olivia," the Lady continued, turning to her eldest twin. "If he is an honourable man, you might contrive to get him alone for a kiss. In a library, perhaps."

Elizabeth nearly choked on her coffee.

"And then he would have to wed you." Lady Weatherstone glanced at Elizabeth, lifting a thin brow. "Are you alright? If you are ill, perhaps you should remain confined in your room. The girls cannot afford to catch ill before the ball."

Elizabeth shook her head.

"Is Miss Elizabeth to attend the ball?" Rose asked.

"She will be present with the other servants, to assist your sisters. Elizabeth, make sure you wear the dark blue dress. We would not want anyone to mistake you for a lady."

Rose's eyes lit up. "Oh, but she must have a gown, Mother!"

Lady Weatherstone waved a pale hand. "Don't be ridiculous. Servants don't wear gowns."

Elizabeth became increasingly certain the woman was toying with her. There was a look in her eyes, an air about her that warned Elizabeth that Lady Weatherstone. . .knew something. And would make trouble.

"Your mother is quite correct," Elizabeth said. "My blue will be quite serviceable. I am here to work, not to dance." She smiled placidly, even though her heart sank a little. What would it have been like to dance with Darcy, be held in his arms?

Well, there would be other balls and other nights, especially if she was to be his wife.

Olivia stood up. "I'm going back upstairs to rest. It doesn't matter what Miss Elizabeth wears, anyway. It's a masquerade ball; everyone will have on masks."

Elizabeth blinked. That was. . .true.

Phoebe followed and Elizabeth rose, but Lady Weatherstone stopped her.

"Miss Elizabeth, pray follow me. I'd like a word."

Elizabeth wondered what new task she was now being asked to administer. Already today, she had acted as both a nurse and a maid to Olivia. Her responsibilities seemed to expand elastically. She would be likely asked to tenderize the next meal.

She followed Lady Weatherstone's to the library. Her employer pursed her lips as she shut the door. "You are not to go anywhere else until I return."

If she was going to be held captive, at least it was around books. After a moment, Elizabeth listened at the door, and hearing nothing, went to peruse the bookshelves. She pulled a book of Marcus Aurelius' Meditations and sat down to leaf through it on the loveseat.

After several minutes, clattering sounds came from the main hall, as though a party arrived and several sets of footsteps came down the floor. Elizabeth turned the page.

Remember that neither the future nor the past pains you, but only the present, she read. She had forgotten how much she liked Aurelius.

Despite her heavy heart, the words seared her, reminding her how much she enjoyed discussing Aurelieus' work with her father. *"Aurlieus is a curmudgeonly old friend,"* her father had said when he introduced her to his work. *"You will like him. He is compassionate but does not suffer fools."* She had always liked that description of him. Much like Papa.

"Very good," Lady Weatherstone said. "Now, let us have our chat." She closed the library door behind her.

"Yes, Lady Weatherstone?"

The older woman took a chair, her languid air sharpening. "Do you know how I spent last night?"

"I'm sorry, I do not." Though she could imagine.

"I had a headache, and I chose to sit in solitude after dinner to alleviate it."

Elizabeth clasped her hands to conceal their faint trembling. She had nothing to fear. But she still, somehow, felt like a mouse about to be caught by a feral cat. "I am sorry that you suffer, ma'am."

Lady Weatherstone smiled mirthlessly. "I get headaches occasionally. Do you know where I go when I get them?"

"I'm sure I don't."

"Why here, in the library, Miss Elizabeth."

Elizabeth's throat went dry.

Lady Weatherstone stood slowly. "You came highly recommended, and my servants have given me good reports of your conduct. I suppose were I a gentlewoman in your position, I would take advantage of any opportunity as well." She narrowed her eyes. "But let this be a warning, Miss Elizabeth. Stay in your place. Any further attempts to seduce one of my guests and I will see you thrown out, your reputation in ruins so the only work you are fit for is that on a street corner. And I will see that the gentleman involved is made a laughingstock."

The threat disturbed her more than the lady knew. Not for her own sake, but for Darcy's. His name dragged through the mud. . .Georgiana's chances to marry her love ruined. No, Elizabeth could not be the cause of that. "So you eavesdropped instead of making your presence known."

"You forget yourself," was the soft, sharp reply. "Do you truly think Darcy is going to make you mistress of Pemberley? He will marry a titled woman who knows his world. He will protect his name and his fortune. What will you choose, Elizabeth? Gratitude for your position, or ruin?"

Elizabeth stood, lowering her head. She would not give Darcy up for anything. . .but she could play the game until it was time to run away. She would warn

Darcy of Lady Weatherstone's threats. But—what could he do if the lady decided to blacken both their names in revenge once she learned Darcy and Elizabeth were betrothed?

And it hit Elizabeth, again, that she was *not* betrothed to Darcy. Not yet. She was making assumptions. Gambling on words he had yet to speak. And till he spoke them. . .

She must be wise. "I am very grateful for my position, Lady Weatherstone. And it would please me to see your daughters well matched."

Lady Weatherstone studied her a moment, then nodded. "You are a sensible sort of girl. I speak for your own good. Even if Darcy were to defy his family and marry you, he would come to regret it and despise you. You would drag his family name down and hurt his sister's reputation."

Elizabeth curtsied. "If you'll excuse me, I should attend to your daughters."

Outside the door, her legs shook. She must speak with Darcy as soon as possible. She must know where they stood.

CHAPTER SIXTEEN

*E*lizabeth reminded herself with each step that the thin soles of her satin slippers were designed for walking indoors, not on the stone steps leading to the garden.

Slap, slap, slap. She strode to a brisk rhythm in her head.

The only way she could think through her troubles was to walk.

The day was bright and cool, the garden mercifully deserted of guests. The air was brisk, the sunshine bright, and she had the large garden to herself.

Still, she fumed silently.

Lady Weatherstone had no right to eavesdrop on her conversation with Darcy.

Lady Weatherstone was her employer and could do as she wished.

Both were true, though contradictory, and it frustrated her deeply.

A flock of birds rose overhead as she made her way from the house. Ogden Hall's garden was not extremely large, but it was well tended and provided a lovely naturescape, even when one was cross.

She passed towering pine trees and made her way to the small, neatly cut replica of the Hampton Court maze Lady Weatherstone had recreated. She stepped behind a stone wall flowering with rose bushes. The maze blocked the wind and the sudden silence surprised her.

Elizabeth was tired of running away from disapproving people. Since her father's death, it seemed as though the doors of society had slammed shut and people around her had grown meaner. Elizabeth knew it was because her family's position had slid further down society's rungs of respectability. But others had it much worse, of course. The shrub wall in front of her rustled and she startled. Then, nothing.

Perhaps it was a bird.

She relaxed and pulled her skirts up her calves to inspect her now damp slippers.

Mud caked the pink satin.

Blast. A perfectly decent pair ruined. Her father would have suggested she needed to better control her emotions, so she didn't fling herself into situations that cost her something as dear as shoes.

A man cleared his throat, and she nearly jumped out of her skin.

Darcy stood in front of her, fully viewing her slim ankles.

Elizabeth dropped her skirts. "Darcy."

The slightest of smiles curved his lips. "My apologies," he said gravely. "I said your name twice and you didn't respond." He paused. "I confess I have been waiting for you. I was told you often walk this way."

Her heart beat faster as they stared at each other. She took a step forward and then another. The third step and she found herself in his arms, his lips on hers in a desperate kiss.

"Elizabeth," he groaned. "We are always interrupted, so this time I shall dispense with pleasantries. Make me the happiest man. Marry me."

"Marry you," she whispered, her hands rising to his face. Then she closed her eyes. "But—"

"No buts, by God."

She opened her eyes. "Are you sure? If my situation and family were beneath you before, then certainly now—"

Darcy's eyes darkened. "I care nothing for your situation. Were you a scullery maid, I would still love you. Do you think a man travels across a country in a mad rush if he cares about. . .situation?"

She laughed softly, the joy in her heart blossoming. "I think Lady Weatherstone will be very vexed. She warned me away from you. She threatened to ruin both our reputations."

He lifted an eyebrow, arrogance glinting in his eyes. "Ask me how little I care for Lady Weatherstone's threat. If she attempts to follow through on her blackmail, she will soon learn the error of her actions." His voice was chilly. "My family is not without resources."

She pursed her lips. "How is Miss Darcy? I ask because there was some concern that any brush of scandal would negatively impact her betrothal."

Darcy grimaced. "It pleases me that you care so much for my sister, but for once you should worry about your own interests."

"Why. . .you make me sound like a social climber."

He closed his eyes briefly. "Be a social climber for once, Lizzy. This one time. Be as good a friend to yourself as you are to Georgiana and I."

She hesitated. "And it is not just friendship that makes you speak?" He had said nothing of love, after all. Perhaps he simply considered her the suitable choice—and she could absolutely see him chasing her across the country for the sake of honour. That he desired her as well, she had no doubt. But none of that was love.

Darcy must have read the thoughts on her face. "Elizabeth Bennet, if this is all for friendship, I am being badly used. You know that I have admired you greatly for some time. You are my first consideration in the morning and my last breath at night. I will not deny my love for you any longer."

He kissed her firmly. "There," he said when he finally let go of her. "Is that what you call friendship?"

It took her two tries to speak. "No."

He narrowed his eyes. "No?"

"No, that is not what I call friendship." Elizabeth stood on her slippered toes, looked into his maddening eyes, and kissed him back.

He stiffened, and his lips took over as he pulled her in for more, arms tightening around her. They could have spent all day like that, but he said, "In case you think it has slipped my notice, you have not yet accepted me."

Elizabeth laughed, sliding her arms around his neck. "Yes. Of course, yes. But. . .what shall I tell the girls? I have grown to love them already." She sighed. "I would have been happy here."

For some perverse reason, the tension in Darcy's body relaxed. "Has Weatherstone treated you well?"

She widened her eyes. "Very well. I do not think I could have done better. I would have been privileged far more than most to have lived the years of my life here. I hope she does not think me ungrateful for choosing marriage over my position."

"Any woman would. She might not like it, but she will understand."

Elizabeth reluctantly stepped away from him. "We

cannot linger if we wish to choose the time and manner of our announcement. The girls frequently walk this way and I would not have them force our hand because they witness something seemingly improper."

His fingers caressed her cheek. "Richard is as giddy as a schoolgirl to attend this ball for some reason that he refuses to admit to me. Do you mind very much if we leave in the morning rather than now?"

Elizabeth laughed. "I had not expected to leave even that soon."

"There is no reason to delay. And every reason for haste. I have a mind to procure a special license in London," he added in a dark mutter.

The undisguised desire in his eyes brought heat to her cheeks. "Patience, Darcy. We have time. We are together now, and there are no more obstructions or misunderstandings. But we must tell Lady Weatherstone. Allow me to choose the best time and I will send word."

He kissed her hand. "As long as it is today, my love."

Darcy watched Elizabeth walk away, old frustration eased only to be replaced by new. She was here, she was his. No one could take her away from him, and there would be—as she said—no further obstructions or misunderstandings. But his body burned for her, and besides that he ached to get back to his life, to begin again with Lizzy at his side. There was also the matter of Georgiana's wedding to see to. It pleased him greatly that she would have a sister to speak to her of feminine things before she wed.

For Darcy intended no delay before he and Elizabeth were made man and wife. They could throw a grand ball later. As soon as they were in London, he would obtain the special license and they would marry.

He followed Elizabeth's path slowly back towards the house. He would speak to Lord Weatherstone, man to man, and let him know Darcy would be taking Elizabeth as his bride and she should be accorded all due courtesy while she remained under this roof, if even only for another day. He would also ask the man to be discreet with the knowledge that Elizabeth had been companion to his daughters here. Darcy had not lied—he did not care if she had been a scullery maid. There was no shame in her supporting herself the way impoverished gentlewomen often had to do. But he wished no unnecessary difficulty for Elizabeth when they were required to socialise.

As he walked, he came upon one of the young ladies of the house. Lord Weatherstone's oldest daughter. . .Ophelia? No, Olivia.

She stood by a flowering bush and glanced over as

his footsteps neared. There was no surprise in her face and he was instantly aware, through the experience of years, that she had been waiting for him. Or another gentleman, perhaps.

"Miss Olivia," he said and bowed, a good distance from her. This was the second day of the house party and he had conversed with her and her sisters briefly.

She curtsied and smiled sweetly. "Mr Darcy, if I recall correctly?"

She knew who he was. So. . .she would be one of *those.* But she was young, and Elizabeth seemed fond of her charges.

"You recall correctly," he said. "Miss Elizabeth recently came along this path. Did you see her?"

Her smile didn't waver, her gaze trained on his. "Oh, I must have missed her." She drew closer. "Are you looking forward to the ball, Mr Darcy? I have high hopes for the evening."

"I am certain it will be very well done."

"You must ask me to dance."

He lifted a brow briefly. She was bold. And assured of her loveliness, which meant spoiled as well. "I do not dance often, but I will be certain for a set."

Darcy made to move around her, but she shifted subtly, barring him. "My father does not enjoy these affairs much either. You and he are much of the same mind, I think. My parents often slip away for a few moments of peace." She flashed a winsome smile. "Perhaps we should follow their example. When the dancing tires you, you must signal, and I will rescue you."

He did not allow himself to smile because it would only encourage her. But she *was* a charming girl. "I think if I should allow any lady to rescue me," he said in a gentle tone, "it would be Miss Elizabeth."

"Miss Elizabeth."

There was no point in prevarication. "She and I have an understanding. We are to discuss it with your mother today. I hope you will forgive me for taking her from you."

She stared at him.

"And I hope," he added, "you will do us the favour of keeping this information to yourself until the appropriate time."

"Of course, Mr Darcy. Congratulations. I should have known Miss Elizabeth would not be with us long."

Darcy bowed and left her, wondering if it was a thread of envy or disappointment he heard in Miss Olivia's voice. But in the end, it did not matter.

Elizabeth floated down the halls of the family wing when a slender, middle aged woman in a well made but simple blue dress poked her head out of a door.

"Miss Elizabeth." She halted. It was Madson, companion to Lord Weatherstone's mother-in-law. "The Lady wishes to speak with you."

It was a peculiarity of this household that they all addressed the snowy haired elderly noblewoman as the Lady. Elizabeth didn't know her well, but she'd seemed a kindly woman. A little eccentric and given to speaking her mind, but kind. Elizabeth entered the room. It was hard to focus on anything but Darcy. Their passion in the maze, the upcoming conversation with Lady Weatherstone and daydream of her new life. But she was still employed for at least another day or two, and she would take her duties seriously.

The Lady smiled warmly, beckoning her closer. She sat at a small table in front of a tall window in her sitting room. "Good afternoon, dear."

Elizabeth curtsied. "Ma'am."

"Sit, girl, don't stand there at attention like a soldier." She waited until Elizabeth obeyed, then said, "I am hiding here from all the flurries over the ball. God help us all if all *her* daughters are not wed to rich dukes by the end of the evening." She rolled her eyes. Madson rolled a tea cart into the room, shutting the door behind her, and began to serve. "Just toast, Madson. Dry toast and strong tea, no sugar."

Elizabeth smiled politely. "Every mother wants the best for her children."

The dowager snorted, lively eyes shrewd. Elizabeth

thought she must have been a most charming woman in her day. Charming, and entirely used to getting her own way. "You must rest too, so you save your strength for dancing. There are young men afoot."

Elizabeth did not know whether the Lady was teasing her, or serious. She erred on the side of courtesy, regardless. She sensed no malice, but perhaps only a certain flouting of conventions. The dowager was old enough not to care as much about societal norms.

"Dancing is not in my cards. But I will be happy to watch over the girls." Elizabeth yearned to dance with Darcy, but did not see how that could be accomplished. Too many people here knew her as the girls' companion. Not as Darcy's betrothed.

"Nonsense. All young unmarried ladies must dance. It is their duty. Even us married and widowed ladies should dance when we can."

Elizabeth opened her mouth to reply and was cut off.

"And give me none of that governess nonsense. You are a young, beautiful woman and a gentleman's daughter. You must be smart. Unless your ambition is to live under my daughter-in-law's thumb until Rose is out, and then be tossed aside, you will seize whatever opportunities you have. In fact, you will *make* opportunities."

If only the dowager knew. Elizabeth coughed a

little. "Ahhh. . .very sensible, ma'am." She had not known till now that the dowager had even noticed her, much less given her situation this much thought.

A welcoming image of standing in Darcy's arms flickered in her mind for a moment. Surely it would not hurt. . .perhaps if Lady Weatherstone permitted it after they spoke to her. But would that not be selfish? It would certainly set tongues to wagging.

Elizabeth cleared her throat and rose. "In any case, I have nothing suitable to wear, ma'am." The fact which settled the issue more than anything else. She had not brought ball gowns with her, and she would not shame Darcy. She curtsied as the dowager pursed her lips. "Please excuse me, I must find the girls."

The Lady waved her off after a moment, turning to her tea. Elizabeth had a feeling the subject wasn't closed.

CHAPTER SEVENTEEN

*L*ady Weatherstone had planned outdoor activities, of course, and Darcy did his duty as an impromptu guest and attended, but his gaze continued to follow Elizabeth as she shepherded her charges. She was not so finely dressed as the other ladies, but her beauty and bearing outshone them all.

"There is an edge of a different kind about you," Richard murmured close to his ear. "Come, cousin. Confess all. You have been staring at Miss Elizabeth this entire time."

Darcy glanced around to ensure they were far enough away from any other guests they could not overhear and pitched his voice low to match Richard's.

"We spoke. She has agreed to become my wife."

Richard slapped him on the back. "Congratulations, cousin. You have finally secured your lady."

"A little quieter, if you please. We have not spoken to Lady Weatherstone yet, and Elizabeth insists."

Richard snorted. "*That* one will not be at all pleased the companion snatched such an eligible bachelor away from her daughters out from under her nose."

"We had a prior relationship. It is not the same thing. I will be certain she understands that there was *never* any hope of a marriage between myself and one of her daughters."

Richard eyed Elizabeth, or perhaps the cluster of ladies surrounding Weatherstone's daughters. "You have found your wife. I am of a mind to find mine."

"Oh?" Darcy followed Richard's gaze, trying to ascertain which lady had captured it.

"I have something in mind. But first, I must go and congratulate my new cousin."

"Not here," Darcy hissed.

"I will be discreet." Mirth danced in Richard's gaze. "And I believe your lady is signaling you anyway."

They approached, and Darcy contrived to stand close to Elizabeth, who whispered to him, "I asked Lady Weatherstone to speak to her about something important and she has just told me she has a few moments now while the guests are occupied. We should..."

"Yes," he said. "Now."

Darcy glanced at Richard, who was teasing Miss

Olivia, and gave him a significant look. 'Good luck', his cousin mouthed.

Darcy wandered after Elizabeth after a few moments. He had no desire to be the subject of gossip at this house party, so they would still behave with circumspection. He followed Elizabeth's path into the house and heard the murmurs of feminine voices. Approaching, he halted in the threshold of a sitting room that overlooked the grassy lawn and current guests. Elizabeth stood in front of Lady Weatherstone and glanced toward him when he cleared his throat.

"Mr Darcy," she murmured.

Lady Weatherstone turned her head, eyebrow rising, and smiled. "Mr Darcy. How are you enjoying the day?"

"Very well, thank you." He looked at Elizabeth, tilting his head slightly to ask if she preferred to do the talking, or should he.

She squared her shoulders. "Lady Weatherstone, Mr Darcy and I have something to discuss with you."

The woman was no fool. She turned suddenly cold eyes on Elizabeth, waiting.

Darcy stepped into the room, approaching the ladies. "It is entirely my fault. Miss Elizabeth has expressed her growing love for your lovely daughters, and her contentment in your household."

"It was a happy chance that Mr Darcy should travel here with his cousin," Elizabeth continued. "And, well.

. .I will speak plainly. He and I were betrothed years ago. There was some difficulty, and the understanding fell through."

"But in recent times we have renewed our acquaintance," Darcy said. "I had planned to ask Miss Elizabeth for her hand again, but she left for London, not knowing my intentions."

"And you happened to come here with your cousin," Lady Weatherstone said. "How fortuitous."

"Indeed," he said.

"If I had had any idea of Mr Darcy's esteem, I should never have taken a position, of course," Elizabeth said. "I am aware it is an inconvenience. But having decided to wed—"

Lady Weatherstone held up a hand. "If you are going to tell me that you plan to leave within the day or even week, I would ask you to reconsider." Her voice was steel. "Of course I would not stand in the way of your happiness, but I would like time to arrange for an alternate companion for my daughters."

"I—" Elizabeth paused, then inclined her head. "Of course."

Darcy barely restrained a shout of frustration.

"I hope you are not too disappointed by the delay," Lady Weatherstone said sweetly.

"Of course not." He bowed.

"And I understand it is awkward for your future bride to be a servant in my household," the lady continued in a suddenly honeyed voice. "I shall be discreet and say nothing to avoid the possibility of any embarrassment."

He stared at her coldly, then inclined his head. She was up to something; there was no acknoweldgement of her threat to Elizabeth. To repay the not quite subtle barb, Darcy walked toward Elizabeth and took her hand, lifting it to his lips to press a gentle kiss on her knuckles.

"There is not another woman in all of England with Miss Elizabeth's grace and beauty who I could consider to take as my wife," he said. "I have waited this long, I can wait a little longer." He lowered her hand and turned to Lady Weatherstone. "And perhaps one day you and your daughters will be guests at Pemberley." An estate vastly superior to hers.

Her mouth tightened, but she gave him another false smile. Darcy took temporary consolation in her displeasure. And began counting the days until he and Elizabeth could leave.

***

Elizabeth fled the room ahead of Darcy, shamelessly avoiding his displeasure. He had pressed the most sensual of kisses on her hand while giving her the most irate of looks. Clearly, he had desired they be off as soon as possible. She understood the source of his impatience. Thinking of it caused her to blush.

"Miss Elizabeth."

Elizabeth, having stepped back outside, turned her head. Olivia stood several feet away, right outside the window of the room where Elizabeth, Darcy, and Lady Weatherstone had just spoken.

"Miss Olivia." Elizabeth approached. "Have you need of me?"

"I overheard your discussion with my mother," the girl said bluntly. "You are Mr Darcy are betrothed, and you mean to leave us."

Elizabeth sighed. "I had hoped to tell you myself. I thought I would be with you girls for some time to come, and found myself quite happy at the prospect."

"I understand, Miss Elizabeth. No gentlewoman would choose to live as a companion when she can be mistress of her own household, especially as wife to a man like Mr Darcy. My congratulations."

Elizabeth stiffened, for a moment hearing a thread of something in Olivia's voice that was not happy congratulations. But then it was gone, and she chose to ignore any possible ill feelings. Not only did it not matter in the long run, but some disgruntlement was to be expected, after all.

Elizabeth smiled and thanked her. "Lady Weatherstone has asked me to remain until you have a new companion."

"My mother respects you a great deal. She is constantly telling me I should be more like you."

"Why—how interesting." She was taken aback. "But that is not so strange. A companion should be an example and I am older than you."

Olivia smiled prettily. "Not so old. You have secured one of the most eligible gentlemen at the party."

Elizabeth began to feel as if she was in a bog. "Well, Mr Darcy and I have known each other for some time now. We are old friends."

Olivia shrugged. "No matter. I suppose I shall have to listen to mother go on and on about how Miss Elizabeth found herself a suitable husband and was not even trying. Should we return to the others?"

***

Olivia fled to the maze, the same place where she had first overheard Darcy and Elizabeth speak of their feelings for each other. She curled her shaking hands into fists.

The *humiliation*—

"Shouldn't you be enjoying your party, Miss Olivia?" a languid male voice said.

She whirled and glared. It was *him*, Mr Darcy's cousin, the one who looked at her as if he could see every petty and uncharitable thought she had about Elizabeth—and that those thoughts only amused him.

"Why are you here?" she demanded. "I wish to be alone."

That he was an eligible bachelor was irrelevant. She would never marry him—he would not at all be a biddable husband, he was far too perceptive. Mr Darcy, with his distant, perfect manners, would have been ideal. The kind of husband who would visit her on occasion in order to get an heir and otherwise leave her to her own devices. Colonel Fitzwilliam would poke and prod at her incessantly.

He stepped forward, a knowing look in his eyes. He was really quite handsome. But far too troublesome. Mama had always said to marry well, and marry a man who you could control.

"I was here first," he said, "but no matter. Tell me, why are you upset? I can always tell when a beautiful woman is about to cry."

She inhaled, glaring at him. "I am about to do no such thing! You are far too familiar, sir."

"I think I can guess," he replied. "I have watched you watch my cousin since we arrived. Perhaps you have heard his happy news?"

She just looked at him coldly. She refused to be baited.

"Happily for you, if Darcy is otherwise occupied at the ball, I will not be."

"Miss Elizabeth is not attending as a guest," she snapped, "so she will hardly be dancing with Mr

Darcy." Olivia then realised her mistake. She had all but confirmed the source of her upset.

Colonel Fitzwilliam smiled. "I claim the first dance now. Do not forget. I am of a mind to claim more than a dance. Perhaps you may find consolation for your bruised heart in me."

Olivia turned on her heels and fled, his mocking laughter following her.

She suppressed her anger the rest of the day, and into the evening. Miss Elizabeth had retired to her room for the night when Mama entered her room.

The maid continued brushing her hair as Lady Weatherstone stood for several long moments, watching. Olivia braced herself, though it did not show on her face.

"Well, it seems Miss Elizabeth has taken for herself one of the wealthiest man among my guests," Mama said, voice cold. "Apparently my eldest daughter was not even in the running. I am hardly surprised. I hired Miss Elizabeth so you could emulate her poise and manners, but you still carry yourself like an urchin. No wonder Mr Darcy would not even consider you. We shall have to set our sights on a lesser man."

"Miss Elizabeth said she and Mr Darcy had a prior understanding, Mama," Olivia said, her voice steady. She had learned long ago that if she showed any of her hurt, it would only prolong her mother's complaints.

"Men are fickle. Had you put yourself in his path

and shown yourself to be superior in every way, he would have turned his attention to you. But he instead chose an old, spinster companion to be his wife over my daughter." Mama's lip curled.

Olivia did not point out that Elizabeth, by her mother's own words, was not old and was beautiful as well, and abandoned any attempts to defend herself and simply endured the rest of the rant. It was not as if she had not heard it all before.

She could not help the growing kernel of resentment towards Elizabeth. It was safe to hate her, for she had no power to make Olivia's life miserable.

*E*lizabeth was not a lady's maid, but it was understood she would assist the girls with their preparations for the ball. And she did not mind. It reminded her of times she and her sisters had crowded together in their rooms to dress—much less sumptuously—and argue over whose hair the maid would do first. The maid tended to do her best job on the first few girls, and was always rushed by the time it was the last sister's turn. Elizabeth had often done her own hair for the sake of expediency.

Olivia was beautiful, though unconventionally so, like Elizabeth. If she hadn't had her own happiness to cradle close, Elizabeth might have been jealous of the swaths of moonlit fabric that composed Olivia's gown. The silvery blue hue set off her dark hair and alabaster skin to perfection. Her mask was a dark blue edged in silver lace and pearls.

Phoebe wore deep rose, which suited her lighter brown hair and blue eyes. The girls had done everything they could to differentiate themselves, and, of course, they were not identical twins.

Olivia rose from her dressing table. "Miss Elizabeth, I spoke to my grandmother earlier. She informed me she ordered you to attend the ball, and not as a companion?" Olivia arched an eyebrow.

"She is very kind. But I have nothing suitable to wear."

"She said you would say that." She nodded at her maid, who left then returned with an armful of gowns. "We are of a similar height and figure. Most of these gowns I have worn only once. I do not think mother will recognise any of them should you choose one."

Elizabeth stared at the pile, startled. "That is very kind of you, but I couldn't. I am quite happy to—"

"Grandmother insists."

"I see. But Lady Weatherstone is expecting me to be present to assist you and Miss Phoebe."

Phoebe waved a hand. "Oh, we'll all be in masks, mother will never know. Just give in, Miss Elizabeth. My grandmother and my sister will have their way. And it will be fun."

"Lady Weatherstone will be looking for me," Elizabeth tried again.

"Not the whole evening," Olivia replied, mouth thinning in a stubborn line. "Appear in your governess dress, make yourself visible, and when she loses interest slip away and get dressed. If we time it right you will make the dancing, then be able to change back before midnight."

It felt duplicitous. Elizabeth pursed her lips. But it was not as if she had to worry about her position. She and Darcy were to be married. It was wrong of Lady Weatherstone to insist she attend the ball as a governess when she knew Elizabeth was Darcy's betrothed. Her conscience, therefore, could endure the small deception.

"Very well," Elizabeth said, trying not to grin. It wouldn't do to seem too giddy. "I will never forget your kindness."

Which surprised her, in a way. She had thought for certain Olivia was still angry. The girl hadn't spoken to her since learning of the betrothal, and Elizabeth had resigned herself to Olivia's silence for the next several days. But evidently Elizabeth's thoughts had been too uncharitable.

Elizabeth took the dresses to her room. She and Olivia *were* much the same size, she realised as she tried on the first of the gowns. Elizabeth's hips and bust were slightly fuller, but she fit the borrowed gowns well enough. It occurred ot her she would need a plain mask as well but perhaps she could fashion one quickly. Her hair was slightly darker than Olivia's, and the girl's eyes were more a dark greyish brown than Elizabeth's true brown, but gowned and masked Lady Weatherstone might not recognise Elizabeth. She would not be looking for her amongst the guests anyway.

She couldn't wear the red one. Her barely concealed bosom burst forth from the low neckline in a way that wouldn't at all do for a governess. She set the dress on the bed and contemplated the remaining two. One was brown—not her colour—while the last was yellow.

The yellow dress was a better fit—thank goodness —and was slightly more modest. She still would need to be careful not to bend in too low of a curtsy lest gentlemen get an eyeful.

She knocked on Olivia and Phoebe's changing room door and opened it. Both girls stood, swathed in jewels and feathers from top to toe, finishing touches on their hair done.

"Miss Elizabeth," Phoebe said with a grimace. "I cannot sit down. My lacings are too tight. I shall have to spend the entire evening standing, mother says."

Olivia rolled her eyes. "Maybe if you had avoided sweet cakes last week as Mama recommended, you'd be able to sit."

"You look very elegant, Miss Phoebe," Elizabeth said. "And you as well, Miss Olivia."

Olivia smiled, running her hands down her silver dress. "It's from a cunning dressmaker in Paris. He sold it to no one else in England." She turned to Elizabeth, knit her brows together. "That dress will not do, Miss Elizabeth."

Elizabeth fought the urge to pull up the neckline and shrugged. "I like it very much. It will suit me just fine for a few sets of dancing."

But Olivia was shaking her head. "No. I have a better idea. Mama ordered a second dress for me, in case I spilled something on this one, or tore a hem in the dancing. You will wear that one."

Elizabeth blinked, nonplussed first by the idea that Lady Weatherstone had gone to the expense of ordering a backup dress for Olivia, and second by the idea of wearing the same gown as her charge.

"A second dress?"

"It is her phobia," Phoebe said. "When she was out she ruined her gown at a ball and was humiliated. She ordered doubles of all of our most important gowns. Father can afford it."

"I do not think—"

Olivia held up a hand. "I insist. It is only for an hour or two, anyway, so you can dance." She paused. "You protest so much, Miss Elizabeth, one would think you were not looking forward to dancing with a certain gentleman."

"I look forward to it very much. But if we are

dressed and masked alike, someone might mistake us as the same person."

Phoebe giggled. "Oh, what fun could be had."

"I do confess to an ulterior motive," Olivia admitted. "I would like to be able to get away to the library for a rest and sit out some of the sets. Mother is determined I dance twice with every gentleman and snare the richest one." She rolled her eyes. "The Season has not even started."

It was a beautiful dress. A dress she would never have been able to afford, even when her parents were alive. Darcy, if he was already in love with her, would surely fall head over heels in love when seeing her so elegantly attired. And perhaps they could slip away for a moment or two in the moonlight...

For once in her life, could she not be fanciful? A little reckless?

"Very well," she heard herself say. "If you think it would aid you..."

Olivia smiled triumphantly.

Darcy grimaced, suppressing the urge to tug at his cravat. "She insists on staying at least two weeks until Lady Weatherstone can arrange for a new companion."

He wanted to whisk Elizabeth away from here and return to Pemberley at once. The idea of his wife in service. . .but he respected her ethics, and her desire to keep her word. It bode well for how she would help raise their children and manage their estate.

Richard grinned at him. "You have your betrothed, and I believe I will soon have mine."

Darcy paused, his hand on the bedroom door. Richard tossed him his mask. "Oh?"

"My mother insists I find a bride this Season, but I'd rather avoid all that nonsense. There is a perfectly suitable lady here." His smile turned smug. "There is a small wrinkle, but nothing I cannot overcome."

"Are you going to tell me?"

"Not at all," was the cheerful response. "That would be no fun. Just wait till the end of the night, mark my words." He paused. "I have a plan and it will benefit us both. You will have to trust me."

Elizabeth stood in the corner of the swirling crowd of people, trying to determine which of the mask clad gentlemen was Darcy. She didn't see him anywhere, but then the increasingly warm room was packed to the gills with finely dressed gossiping ladies and gentlemen.

She inched her way back behind her two exquisitely dressed charges as a tall, broad shouldered man approached, a gleam in wicked blue eyes. For a moment, she thought he was Darcy.

"Miss Phoebe, allow me the honour of telling you how exquisite you look this evening," the man said, kissing Phoebe's hand. "Miss Olivia, you are also a vision."

Elizabeth recognised the well-modulated tone. His register and inflection were much the same as Darcy's, and perhaps someone who did not know her betrothed as well as she might mistake Richard for his cousin, but Elizabeth never would.

"Sir," Olivia said, flashing a sweet smile.

Elizabeth glanced at her sidelong. Olivia must think it was Darcy. . .let her. That meant when it was Elizabeth's time for dancing, Olivia would be happily occupied. She need never know it was Colonel Fitzwilliam entertaining her.

"And you must tell me how you know who I am, sir," Olivia said, playfully tapping his arm with her fan.

"Your beautiful smile, of course. I would know it anywhere."

He led her towards the dancefloor and Phoebe slipped into the crowd after them and Elizabeth was once again free to visually search for Darcy.

It did not take long for a somberly dressed man, also in a plain black mask, to wander over to her side.

"The lady does not wish to dance?" he asked in a low voice.

Elizabeth replied, barely moving her lips, "The lady is a companion, and not present to dance. As you can see from my dress."

"Ah. But if the dress makes the lady, then perhaps. . ."

She flashed Darcy a brief, conspiratorial smile. She had been able to slip him a note informing him of the evening's scheme.

"Indeed," she said. "Who knows? Perhaps I shall dance this evening after all."

Elizabeth slipped out of the ballroom, taking care to walk unhurriedly. Not that anyone would be paying attention to a companion. Once she was clear of that wing of the house, she dashed toward her modest room, and began the process of changing her gown.

There was a knock on the door, and Elizabeth turned to see Miss Rose slip inside. The youngest of the sisters grinned at her and clapped her hands.

"I have been on the lookout. I will help you change and dress your hair. Hurry, hurry, Miss Elizabeth."

Elizabeth worried for a moment about the wisdom of involving Rose, but the girl's enthusiasm sparked her own. It began to feel like an adventure, and really, there was very little harm in it. It was not as if she had to worry about losing her position. As Rose helped

Elizabeth rearrange her hair into something quick, but more elegant, Elizabeth almost felt as if she was seventeen again and preparing for a ball at Netherfield. Her parents alive, her sisters chattering. Her mother flitting about with hopes of finding her daughter's husbands.

She felt a pang of sadness as she looked at herself in the mirror. Her mother would have been ecstatic. Jane would be as well, but her sister was far away in London. Perhaps once she wed, Darcy would not mind if she invited them all to Netherfield. Not forever, but. . .it had been so long since they were all in a room together.

Banishing the melancholy—there was so much to be grateful for—she kissed Rose on the cheek and slipped back out of the bedroom.

When she entered the ballroom this time, she was magically transformed into a guest. She took a moment to survey the glittering throng. Surely this was the most elegant ball she had ever attended, Netherfield included.

The strain of music drew her forward. Candlelight glimmered, sparkling off ladies' jewels. She weaved through the crowd, looking for that one particular gentleman.

She did not have long to wait.

"May I have the honour of this dance?" a deep voice said behind her.

Elizabeth turned.

Blue eyes stared down at her intently, a small smile hovering over well-shaped lips. He was dressed in shades of blue and black, much like his cousin. She smiled. Exactly like his cousin, if she recalled correctly.

Well, that made sense. Perhaps Darcy had not brought proper attire with him and borrowed some of Colonel Fitzwilliam's. It seemed like she and he both wore borrowed finery tonight. It was so appropriate.

Elizabeth placed her hand in his and allowed him to lead her to the dance floor. She threw herself into the dance. What could Lady Weatherstone do, even if she guessed? Elizabeth trusted Darcy; if he said he could thwart any attempts by the lady to make trouble, she must believe in him.

And she so wanted nothing to spoil this special evening, the night of her betrothal.

After the set, he led her to the punch table. "I long to be alone with you," he murmured in her ear. "Should we take some fresh air?"

He stood almost too close for politeness, but perhaps some of her own wildness had infected him as well.

"Yes," she said, "but let us remain discreet."

His eyebrow quirked. "Of course."

He let her make her way out of the ballroom first.

Moonlight. A cool breeze. Elizabeth inhaled it greedily, relieved to be in the shadows.

Somewhere in the distance, she heard a male and

female voice laugh softly. A clandestine couple had also chosen the garden to get away from the crowds. Thankfully, they weren't near.

The musicians stopped playing. She walked several steps away from the warm light of the house. She had just been here a few days earlier. With him. She marveled at how different it seemed. Each lovely bloom and leaf in the garden had delighted her then.

"Elizabeth."

She turned as Darcy approached. "It seems all we have are these stolen moments." She gave him a tremulous smile.

Darcy took her hands and lifted them to his lips. "You are to be my wife. The moments will not always be stolen."

"Now who is counseling patience?" she teased.

"There are worse things," he said softly, "than courting my bride in a garden in the moonlight. At least this way we have somewhat of a courtship." He drew her closer.

Elizabeth looked up into his masked face. "I do not need one. But you're right. I will enjoy this time and tell the story to our children." A smile curved her lips. "I will even endeavour to make it sound less innocent than it is."

Darcy laughed, a deep, rich sound. "I would not want you to lie to our children, Elizabeth. Allow me to make our evening a little less innocent in truth."

This time his kiss wasn't sweet, wasn't soft. He imbued it with all his frustrated passion, and she returned the kiss with all of her own.

"Miss Elizabeth!"

Elizabeth jerked, startled, and Darcy released her with a sigh. They turned as a young woman came swiftly down the path. The music had struck up again, and the strains floated in the air. Elizabeth had hoped no other guests would come out of the house. She had also hoped her charges would have given her time as well.

"Miss Phoebe," Elizabeth said, then frowned. "What is wrong?"

"Miss Elizabeth, come quickly," Phoebe said. "My mother and sister are up to something despicable!"

Darcy, at Elizabeth's back, said nothing. She glanced over her shoulder quickly to see he had donned his mask and stepped deeper into the shadows.

Phoebe whirled and hustled away, and Elizabeth followed. Darcy walked behind her, footsteps nearly silent.

"Whatever is going on?" Elizabeth muttered to herself.

If Darcy were not at her side, the odd feeling of dread uncurling in her middle would have disturbed her more. She had had a feeling for hours that an ax was about to lop off her head, but as her thoughts raced, she could not for the life of her decide the nature of the ax.

Phoebe led them into the house towards a sitting room near the ballroom. Phoebe paused, glancing back at Elizabeth, then stopped when she saw Darcy.

"Miss Elizabeth, who is this?" Phoebe asked.

"Mr Darcy," Elizabeth said, somewhat hesitantly. "We were getting some fresh air."

Phoebe's eyes widened. "Then who—" she turned back and stared at the slightly ajar door.

It was then Elizabeth heard a murmur of voices within. Phoebe stepped forward, pressing her ear gently against the door. Hand on the knob, presumably so it would not open accidentally.

"Miss Phoebe," Elizabeth said. "Whatever is going on?"

Phoebe lifted a finger to her mouth, peering into the room. After a long moment when Elizabeth was about to demand an explanation more forcefully, Phoebe beckoned her forward.

"Not you, Mr Darcy," the girl said. "Stay out of sight for a moment." So much for his disguise.

Phoebe shoved open the door, and she and Elizabeth stepped into the threshold.

"Miss Olivia!" Elizabeth exclaimed.

The older twin was clasped in the arms of a gentleman. She recognised his profile, even masked, from earlier in the evening.

"Miss Elizabeth!" Olivia cried, then blushed prettily. She glanced up at the man holding her, almost coyly.

Elizabeth grabbed Darcy's hand and drew him inside the room, nudging Phoebe forward, and closed the door. Darcy moved to the side, saying nothing. Olivia glanced at him, hesitated, then turned her attention back to the gentleman as he lifted her hand to his mouth.

"Miss Olivia," she said. "This is inappropriate behaviour. I would like an explanation from *you*, sir." She was angry and did not bother to disguise it. "You are a guest in this home and to behave this way..."

"I am so sorry, Miss Elizabeth," Olivia said in a rush. "I hope we have not disappointed you, I could not bear it. But I guess our feelings just carried us away."

"You know what Mother will do if she catches you," Phoebe said. "We should leave immediately and never speak of this again."

But there was an odd note in Phoebe's voice.

"Will you ever forgive me, Miss Elizabeth?" Olivia asked.

Elizabeth frowned at her. "A lapse in decorum is regrettable, but if we repair quickly to the ballroom, I do not see how—"

The sitting-room door opened. "Olivia!"

Lord and Lady Weatherstone stood in the doorway.

Lady Weatherstone pointed, finger trembling as she pressed a hand to her heaving bosom. "It is as I told you, husband!"

Lord Weatherstone stepped into the room. "An explanation, sir," he said in a hard voice.

"It is quite obvious," the lady snapped. "Mr Darcy has compromised our daughter. He must marry her!"

"What is your answer, Mr Darcy?" Lord Weatherstone demanded. "Will you do the honourable thing?"

"I would always do the honourable thing," Darcy replied. "But I think there may be a misunderstanding."

All heads turned towards Darcy. Lady Weatherstone's eyes widened as she looked between the two gentlemen.

Elizabeth's eyes narrowed. Were there two games afoot this evening? Darcy and his cousin were dressed identically. She had noted to herself before how similar they looked. How was it that Olivia thought Richard was Darcy?

She looked at her betrothed, who met her gaze, his blue eyes calm. There was none of the outrage she might expect at being accused of compromising the daughter of his host.

Elizabeth glared at him. They would have words later.

Lord Weatherstone sputtered as his wife went pale. Olivia jerked away from the gentleman next to her.

"Oh no!" she wailed. "Who are *you?*"

Elizabeth crossed her arms, her anger growing. "What trick is this?"

The gentleman bowed to Lord Weatherstone, and removed his mask. "Sir, I will absolutely do the honourable thing. It would make me deeply happy if Miss Olivia would consent to be my wife." A small smile played around his lips as he looked sideways at an aghast Olivia.

"Never!" She gasped. "Not if—"

"Be silent, daughter," Lord Weatherstone said coldly. "Colonel Fitzwilliam, I must censure you for your behaviour. But if your intentions were honourable and my daughter did not object to your attentions, then I suppose one must forgive the impulsiveness of youth. We will talk, and discuss the particulars in the morning."

Lady Weatherstone was staring daggers at Darcy, who returned her gaze with a lifted brow. She turned on her heel and swept out of the room.

"Well," Phoebe said, "that went very well." Then she laughed.

"Admittedly, my cousin's idea seems less sound in hindsight," Darcy said. "He was to entertain Miss Olivia and allow her to conclude he was, in fact, myself, if she came to that conclusion. So we might have some time together."

She stared at him. "In hindsight. But what he did instead was—"

"Indeed. I will have a discussion with him." But Darcy sounded placid, rather than disapproving.

"You are incorrigible."

He stopped pretending and grinned. "Well, you must admit everything is working out nicely. The girl wanted a husband, and a husband she now has."

"She wanted you."

He shook his head. "She wanted to prove she was the better woman. She only proved she is a child. Her mother, however—" he paused, and Elizabeth saw the flash of anger in his eyes. "My best revenge is to wed you as soon as possible and then flaunt my beautiful bride." The anger faded, or at least turned into another form of heat.

"Well, we must only endure her for another two weeks."

Darcy stared at her. "You must be joking."

"I gave my word. Two weeks, to give her time to find another companion." Elizabeth smiled sweetly. "But it will be two weeks where she must meet me at the breakfast table each morning as I discuss wedding plans with her daughter. And I believe I am done with dressing as befits my station."

Darcy chafed at the delay the entire time, and within a week (as Elizabeth had secretly predicted) Lady Weatherstone released her from her promise and she was off to London with her betrothed.

She had not spent the time idle; several letters had gone out. To Charlotte, to her sisters. Darcy made short work of calling the banns, and it was decided that instead of a hurried ceremony in London, they would travel to Pemberley and wed there, giving her sisters time enough to arrive.

It was at Pemberley she finally met Lord Randolph's parents.

"May I introduce my bride, Miss Elizabeth?" Darcy said when she entered the drawing room. They had arrived late the previous evening and Elizabeth, not wanting to face a duke and duchess quite yet, pleaded fatigue and escaped to her rooms. A knock on the door several minutes later revealed Mrs Frasier, whom Darcy had invited to stay until they were wed.

"My sister is chaperone enough," he informed her later, "but I thought you might enjoy Mrs Fischer's company until your sisters come." A fleeting look of pain crossed his expression, and Elizabeth laughed at him.

"Miss Elizabeth," the duke rumbled, giving her a critical eye.

Her greeting to the duke and duchess was pleasant and restrained. Elizabeth kept her contributions to the conversation to a minimum, exchanging a covert look with Georgiana who seemed to have come to a similar conclusion. Not quite afraid of making a poor impression, but aware the best chance to avoid doing so was simply not to speak overmuch and be proven a fool. It was easier to relax, especially since Caroline had finally returned home—or was asked to leave, Elizabeth was not sure which and Darcy refused to answer.

"Where are you from, Miss Elizabeth?" the duchess asked.

A slender woman of medium height, light brown hair just silvering at the edges, her dress and bearing were understated, her manners perfect. She fussed over her son in a perfunctory way that Randolph endured with a resigned expression.

"Hertfordshire, your grace," she said.

"Do we know anyone in Hertfordshire, dear?" she asked her husband, who grunted. The duchess turned back to Elizabeth. "Have we met your family?"

"I would not think so." She steeled herself to the line of questioning which inevitably led to the correct conclusion that Elizabeth hailed from humble roots. That her family home was currently in the hands of a cousin, and her sisters scattered.

She steered the conversation back to Georgiana's wedding plans and tried to avoid any mention of her own, which would also inevitably lead to a comparison between her family and the Darcy's.

By the end of dinner that evening, though, the duchess nodded to Darcy. "It is so refreshing to see a young man choose a bride for the soundness of the head on her shoulders rather than simple beauty."

"A wife should be an asset to running an estate such as this," the duke said. "A silly girl would just bleed your coffers dry." He cast a critical gaze on Georgiana. "A settled young woman knows her duty. Keep a firm hand with the staff, take care of her husband, bear him heirs. Maintain the dignity of the family name."

Elizabeth took this as a roundabout compliment, and when Georgiana came to her room that night, they laughed over it.

George flung herself on the bed, rolling her eyes. "A woman's place is at home, bearing heirs and keeping the peasants in check," she mocked. "Not in London reading and shopping and getting into trouble. They approve of *you*."

"Has the duke said he does not approve the match with Randolph?"

She grimaced. "I think he is hoping you will influence me. He sees you as settled and traditional and properly submissive to my brother. Ugh."

Elizabeth was a bit at a loss for words. "He gathered all that?"

Georgiana gave her a look. "It is the polite, stoic silence. A woman who does not speak is the essence of femininity."

"I. . .was only trying to avoid any potentially difficult topics." Elizabeth laughed, and Georgiana joined her.

"I suppose I can sit and look pretty for a few days," George concluded, "if that is what it takes. After Randy and I are married, it won't matter anymore. What do you say to a double wedding? The faster we get it done, the better."

However, it was decided that Elizabeth and Darcy should wed at Pemberley, and Georgiana and

Randolph would have a fashionable London wedding —the duchess insisted on that.

"Your modesty does you credit, my dear," the duchess said to Elizabeth, "and so becoming in a woman of your birth. But my only son must wed in London, I am certain you understand. It will be an affair."

Elizabeth murmured agreement and carefully avoided looking at George's pained expression. Darcy's sister would have preferred a quiet wedding at home, but she proved herself a diplomat, as always.

Spring came late to Pemberley that year, but when it finally arrived in late April, it bloomed spectacularly. Even Georgiana agreed the flowers and plants seemed larger and bolder than years past, but—as she noted— his views might be skewed due to his own happiness.

All this meant that Elizabeth and the gardeners ultimately had many magnificent blooms to choose from when decorating Pemberley for the wedding. In the end, they chose simple lilies of the valley to affix to the side of the pews in the chapel, matching the modest bouquet in Elizabeth's hands and the sprig on Darcy's collar.

At the moment, a white pip of a lily had somehow lodged itself in Darcy's hair near his ear.

"What are you doing, Mrs Darcy?" Darcy asked, his eyes warm as Elizabeth leaned across the open landau and plucked the pip from his dark curl.

"You have a flower in your hair," she said. "Unless that was an intentional part of your bridegroom uniform."

Darcy eyed the tiny pip in her gloved fingers and, smiling, shook his head. "No, that was not part of the groomsman attire this year. Flower pips are very last season in terms of wedding fashions."

Elizabeth let the bud fall from her fingers and nestled closer to her new husband.

"A shame. You looked well wreathed in flowers."

"Not as well as you," he said, and despite his usual reserve, he leaned in to kiss his new wife in full view of all their guests as they rode away from the church.

It was the first instance in the years to come where Darcy had surprised villagers by abandoning his disdain of displays of public affection toward his wife.

It would not be the last.

A Limited Edition Winter Compilation

A SECRET SUITOR

A mysterious suitor. Dashing Mr Darcy. A secret stalker poised to snatch Elizabeth Bennet from both. Torn between her secret correspondent and Mr Darcy, Elizabeth must decide if courtship and marriage are even in her future. She does not have time to wait, for Mr Bennet is gravely ill and it is up to her to save the family from poverty—even if it means accepting a position as a governess. A position that brings an unexpected cloud of danger. But Mr Darcy has a secret of his own, and it is time he reveals himself to Elizabeth Bennet—but his revelation may come too late, costing him the only woman he has ever desired to wed.

WHAT LINGERS IN THE HEART

Darcy's secret longing for a woman who will not have him. Elizabeth's determination to marry for love, and not money. An epic battle of wills. . .who will win and who will wed? Five years ago Darcy prevented Lizzy from eloping with their mutual childhood friend Wickham. This time when Darcy intervenes, it will not be just to save Lizzy from herself. . .but to claim the woman he has always considered his as mistress of Pemberley.

PRINCE DARCY

A midnight rescue. Prince Darcy in disguise. A magical gem that marks Elizabeth as a Pemberley bride. . .Prince Darcy of Pemberley did not expect to battle wits and join forces with Miss Elizabeth Bennet of Longbourn. But after a midnight encounter with the mysterious, fiery-eyed beauty leaves him intrigued and desiring to know her better, Darcy almost forgets why he has come in secret to Meryton.

My Darling Darcy is a sweet Pride & Prejudice Variation compilation offered in a Limited Edition winter cover to add to your collection.

Will Darcy lose a battle of wits or his heart?

A stolen kiss in the library...
A distraction he can't shake...

After hearing him says she's "not handsome" at the
Meryton Assembly, Elizabeth knows just enough
about Mr. Darcy not to like him. Called to Netherfield
to nurse Jane back to health, Elizabeth simply wants to
return home to Longbourn.
What she doesn't realize is that he's hopelessly
besotted with her and his poor humor is a result of
trying—and losing—control of his emotions.

An encounter in the library changes all that.

Just as Elizabeth starts to see Darcy's true self, their past and private assumptions threaten their fragile connection.

Mr. Darcy's Distraction is a sweet and (slightly) spicy Pride and Prejudice variation novella of 10,000 words where wits are battled and passions rise.

ABOUT THE AUTHOR

Allison Smith is a work-from-home mother of five who is only semi-accomplished in various arts such as music, jewelry making, and sewing, but feels herself reasonably accomplished at stringing a sentence or two together into a pleasing story.

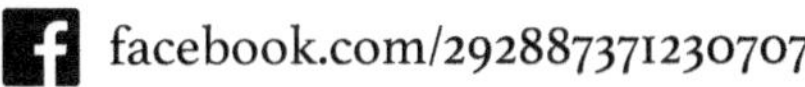 facebook.com/292887371230707

Grace Sellers is a writer, college instructor, lifelong animal lover, and pop culture geek living in Chicago. She is thrilled to have found a use for her love of period movies, history, and literature that doesn't involve lying on the couch and eating ice cream (not that there's anything wrong with that).

She has student loans (and degrees) from University of Wisconsin-Madison and lived there for many years. You can see pictures of her past and present pets on her Facebook page. A good portion of any income she earns will inevitably go to rescue animals. Please do not bring her any needy dogs, cats or horses.

WEBSITE

www.ingramcontent.com/pod-product-compliance
Lightning Source LLC
Chambersburg PA
CBHW070752160726
48004CB00001B/153